"A sense of danger and menace perv٤
lightened by Mad's genuine likabili٦
crafted an extremely unique mystery series with an intelligent
heroine whose appeal will never go out of style."

*– Kings River Life Magazine*

"If you are looking for an unconventional mystery with a snarky,
no-nonsense main character, this is it...Instead of clashing, humor
and danger meld perfectly, and there's a cliffhanger that will make
your jaw drop."

*— RT Book Reviews*

"A terrific mystery is always in fashion—and this one is sleek, chic
and constantly surprising. Vallere's smart styling and wry humor
combine for a fresh and original page-turner—it'll have you eagerly
awaiting her next appealing adventure. I'm a fan!"

*— Hank Phillippi Ryan,*
Agatha, Anthony, and Mary Higgins Clark Award-Winning Author

"Diane Vallere...has a wonderful touch, bringing in the design
elements and influences of the '50s and '60s era many of us hold
dear while keeping a strong focus on what it means in modern
times to be a woman in business for herself, starting over."

*— Fresh Fiction*

"All of us who fell in love with Madison Night in *Pillow Stalk* will be
rooting for her when the past comes back to haunt her in *That
Touch of Ink*. The suspense is intense, the plot is hot and the style is
to die for. A thoroughly entertaining entry in this enjoyable series."

*— Catriona McPherson,*
Agatha Award-Winning Author of the Dandy Gilver Mystery Series

"A multifaceted story...plenty of surprises...And what an ending!"

*— New York Journal of Books*

"A humorous yet adventurous read of a mystery, very much worth considering."

— *Midwest Book Review*

"Make room for Vallere's tremendously fun homage. Imbuing her story with plenty of mid-century modern decorating and fashion tips...Her disarmingly honest lead and two hunky sidekicks will appeal to all fashionistas and antiques types and have romance crossover appeal."

— *Library Journal*

"If you love Doris Day, you'll love Madison Night, decorator extraordinaire. She specializes in restoring mid-century homes and designs, and her latest project involves abductions, murder and vengeance."

– *Books for Avid Readers*

"The characters in this series are really great and you laugh and cry along with them when necessary. Madison and Tex are a terrific pair, and the story will definitely keep readers entertained....and after you're done reading you will very much want to find a Doris Day movie to enjoy as much as this book."

– *Suspense Magazine*

"A charming modern tribute to Doris Day movies and the retro era of the '50s, including murders, escalating danger, romance...and a puppy!"

— Linda O. Johnston,
Author of the Pet Rescue Mysteries

"A well-constructed tale with solid characters and page after page of interesting, intelligent dialogue. Diane Vallere delivers a cunning plot as well as humor and romance."

– *ReadertoReader.com*

# THE DECORATOR WHO KNEW TOO MUCH

**The Madison Night Mystery Series**
**by Diane Vallere**

<u>Novels</u>

PILLOW STALK (#1)

THAT TOUCH OF INK (#2)

WITH VICS YOU GET EGGROLL (#3)

THE DECORATOR WHO KNEW TOO MUCH (#4)

<u>Novellas</u>

MIDNIGHT ICE
(in OTHER PEOPLE'S BAGGAGE)

# THE DECORATOR WHO KNEW TOO MUCH

A Madison Night Mystery

*Diane Vallere*

HENERY PRESS

THE DECORATOR WHO KNEW TOO MUCH
A Madison Night Mystery
Part of the Henery Press Mystery Collection

First Edition
Trade paperback edition | April 2017

Henery Press
www.henerypress.com

Trade Paperback ISBN-13: 978-1-63511-195-8
Digital epub ISBN-13: 978-1-63511-196-5
Kindle ISBN-13: 978-1-63511-197-2
Hardcover Paperback ISBN-13: 978-1-63511-198-9

Printed in the United States of America

*To my fellow Dayniacs*

## ACKNOWLEDGMENTS

Thank you to Ramona DeFelice Long for your valuable feedback on this manuscript, Jane Feuer, for your eagle eye, Kendel Lynn for your friendship, and the whole team at Henery Press for your support of the Madison Night series. And to Josh Hickman, who didn't think it was weird when I looked into the river on a recent vacation and said, "What if there was a dead body in the water?" Sometimes it's nice not to be thought of as weird.

# PROLOGUE

*Tex*

Tex Allen wasn't the sort of guy who spent Saturday nights alone. There was the natural Daddy Complex—something he'd encountered early on in his days as a cop—but the older he got, the more interesting he appeared to be to the opposite sex. The other officers in the precinct called it the Clooney Syndrome. They said the longer he indicated he wasn't interested in a long-term relationship, the more attractive he became to the ladies.

*The ladies*, he thought with a chuckle. A couple of years ago, he would have thought of them as chicks or, worse, girls. That was before he'd met Madison Night. He didn't admit it to most, but ever since the day he'd found her and her Shih Tzu by the edge of the parking lot of Crestwood pool, after finding a corpse under the back tires of her Alfa Romeo, he'd been a changed man. But Madison had started a relationship with Hudson James. Tex wasn't the type to hold anybody's past mistakes against him, but he couldn't help feeling jealous when he thought about Madison shifting from a life she shared with her dog to one she shared with her handyman.

He poured the rest of his beer into his glass and clicked through the channels. No games, no James Bond movies, no *Deadliest Catch* marathons. There was an open invitation for him to join the off-duty Lakewood PD at Jumbo's Strip Club, but he'd been there and done that. He was approaching fifty and, as much as he didn't want to admit it, lately he'd found himself thinking that maybe life was passing him by. Who knew a woman his age in a polyester suit from the sixties would be the one to make him rethink his lifestyle.

Tex finished off his beer and got another. Downtime had been more and more like this: one beer too many, falling asleep in the recliner in front of the TV. As long as the morning pot of coffee got him going before he headed in to work on the latest homicide, he was fine. He'd added in kickboxing and extra rounds at the shooting range so he'd have an outlet for stress. He even sent Christmas cards to his remaining family members this year. And then there was Peter Randall, his one-on-one basketball buddy, who just so happened to also be his psychiatrist. Now instead of going through the motions, he found himself thinking about opportunities lost and doors that had closed. Instead of focusing on doing his job every day, he questioned whether or not he was happy.

Yeah, life for Tex Allen had taken a turn somewhere in the recent past and he wasn't sure how he felt about it.

When he returned to the living room, he found that TCM was running a Doris Day marathon. *Fine*, he thought. *I'm man enough to watch a Doris Day movie.* He finished off his new beer faster than expected and tipped the chair back to a more comfortable angle.

He woke up the next morning with a crick in his neck and a desire to paint the kitchen yellow.

Yep, meeting Madison Night had changed him. For better or worse? He still wasn't sure.

# ONE

If Hudson had gotten his way, I wouldn't have known about the trip to Palm Springs until we arrived at the airport. Perhaps it was the fact that I'd already experienced the frustration of traveling with a suitcase filled with someone else's clothes thanks to a baggage mishap at the airport a few years ago, or that there are some things you'd just rather do for yourself. Either way, his romantic notions of whisking me away with already packed suitcases were thwarted by my naturally inquisitive nature.

"It was a nice idea," I said. "Impractical, but nice."

"It was supposed to be a surprise." Hudson bent down and grabbed my bag from the conveyor belt.

"Maybe I don't like surprises," I said.

"Who doesn't like surprises?"

The kind of person who had lived through more than her share of them.

Hudson James had been my contractor for five years and my leading man for five months. I'd resisted the attraction for as long as I could because his talents had become vital to the success of my decorating business, Mad for Mod. But there was more to life than business, and I'd been pleasantly surprised by how easily we'd merged the various aspects of our individual lives. If only his cat and my dog got along as well as we did, we'd be golden.

"That's all of the luggage," Hudson said.

"Check the tags."

"Madison, exactly how many vintage turquoise Samsonite suitcases do you think are floating around in the world?"

I smiled. "You'd be surprised."

He flipped over the black luggage tag, exposing my pink, yellow, and blue business card. *Madison Night, Mad for Mod.*

"Satisfied?"

"For now."

While Hudson adjusted the stack of suitcases on the rolling cart, I let Rocky out of his carrier and attached his leash. He looked up at me with his large brown eyes. He was a Shih Tzu, small enough that he was allowed to ride in the airplane cabin with the rest of us, but he wasn't used to being cooped up for quite so long. I scooped him up, kissed him, and then set him down. He immediately ran over to Mortiboy's carrier and sniffed. A lazy black kitty paw stretched forward and swatted at Rocky's nose. Mortiboy was under the influence of a veterinarian-prescribed sedative, but that didn't mean he would let Rocky get the wrong idea about which one of them was in charge.

The Palm Springs International Airport was easy to navigate. Within minutes our bags were stacked in the back of a Jeep that had been left in short-term parking. Our trip to Palm Springs was only part getaway; Hudson's brother-in-law owned a construction company and had recruited us to work for him for the next two weeks. The Jeep was part of his fleet of vehicles, and he'd mailed the spare key to Hudson before we left Texas. It was yet another detail that I'd gotten out of Hudson during the three-hour flight. The top to the Jeep was off and it was safe to speak for all of us: in what felt like ninety-degree temperature, the passing breeze was welcome, despite what it did to our hair.

I'd recently acquired the estate of an eighty-nine-year-old woman who'd spent her youth as a fit model for a couple of companies that produced sewing patterns. To hear her daughter tell it, Mom had been hired to try on completed garments to make sure the measurements on the patterns were accurate, and part of her compensation was the opportunity to buy said garments at annual sample sales. Hidden amongst the various blankets and sheets sets in her linen closet were deep plastic bins of items that appeared to have been worn once, if at all. Each perfectly coordinated outfit had been packed in a sealable plastic bag with the corresponding pattern. Today's ensemble was Simplicity 6013, a sleeveless A-line tunic with high slits on either side and coral, mint green, and white striped Bermuda shorts underneath. I paired it with coral canvas sneakers, my footwear option of choice.

"Tell me again about the project that brought us to Palm Springs in September? It's not exactly tourist season."

"That's part of the reason why we're here," Hudson said. He grinned. "You never did strike me as one to do the expected."

"If you can take it, so can I." I reached my hands up and pushed my blonde hair away from my face. "Give me a day to adjust and then I'll be fine."

He slowed for a red light and kissed me on the cheek. "I love your adventurous spirit."

"Is that what you call it? I call it a job," I said playfully.

"The job. Right." He laughed. "It should have been a vacation. You need one. This was the only way to get you out of town."

I reached over and took his hand. Hudson was right; I had a tendency to throw myself into work and the past few months had been no exception. When he'd first mentioned his sister's husband was working on a mid-century modern-inspired project in Palm Springs, it had been my curiosity, not my need for a paying, out-of-state job, that interested me.

"You said your brother-in-law has been planning this for a long time—something about a themed strip mall? What is it we'll be doing?"

"This has been Jimmy's dream. He's been acquiring wreckage from old buildings around the outskirts of Palm Springs for a couple of years now, and he just bought a parcel of land that he plans to develop into a strip mall. We're talking stuff that's been laying around since the fifties. When he first got the idea, it was to buy signs and fixtures cheap and resell to developers, but so much of Palm Springs is rooted in mid-century style and the Rat Pack era that he invested in his own properties. We're here to help him build and renovate what he bought. When we're done he'll rent them out."

"Isn't that a little backward? Don't most rental companies rent out space and allow their tenants to fixture and sign them as they see fit?"

"That's exactly his selling point. His strip mall will be totally cohesive. He's hoping to make it a destination spot by incorporating history into his design. He filed a petition to remove some of the old, weathered external signs from abandoned businesses in Salton Springs and they're going to restore them and use them here. I'm going to help him with the building and construction, and you can help with the decorating."

"So it's going to be authentically mid-mod but new."

"That's the idea. Palm Springs has always been a tourist town. It's in the middle of the desert. Why would you come here? To get away. Real estate is pretty cheap, but a lot of people only live here November to April because the temperature gets to be too hot the rest of the time."

I fanned myself with my hand. "I hadn't noticed."

"Jimmy thought we'd be able to take it because we're used to living in Texas. The temperature is the same there as it is here."

"I don't know if I've gotten used to living in Texas."

"Come on. I thought you said you were adaptable."

"You're right. I think the heat gave me temporary amnesia."

Hudson consulted some directions he'd written on a sheet of printer paper and turned left onto a narrow road. He slowed significantly and we crawled along, passing ranch house after ranch house. I forgot about the temperature, absorbed in the architecture around us. Mid-century style—decorating, clothing, cars, and architecture—was my passion. I'd fallen in love with the look thanks to a steady diet of the Doris Day movies my parents had bought me on my birthday every April third. The actress and I shared more than a birthday. After my parents died in a car accident while I was in college, I'd turned to Doris Day as a role model. She'd experienced her own share of adversity, but remained positive and charming through it all. I'd never once heard of her viewing herself as a victim, and that was the way I wanted to live. So Doris became my guide, and I set about creating the kind of world that she lived in.

In a world that was growing ever more casual, I knew that dressing in sixties vintage made me different, but truth was, I was more comfortable in a polyester skirt suit than if I'd worn jeans and a tee. I could hardly remember a time when I looked like everybody else. It had started with a miniskirt here, a capelet there. It wasn't a stretch to see how her style had morphed into mine.

I'd built my whole decorating business around the aesthetic I saw in her movies too. Through the slightly morbid business model of reading the obituaries to identify estates that were likely filled with the kind of items I'd need, I amassed a collection of original (though sometimes in need of TLC) inventory to use in future jobs. Buying estates in whole had the secondary benefit of giving me first dibs at vintage clothes and accessories, which suited my lifestyle.

The Jeep bumped along the narrow road, occasionally swaying from side to side thanks to the uneven terrain. Hudson handed me the sheet of paper. "I recognize where we're at. Emma and Jimmy's house should be just up the street."

"Great. I'm pretty sure Mortiboy's sedative is wearing off. If we don't get there soon, I'm afraid he's going to start plotting revenge against me for keeping him in his cat carrier while Rocky has his freedom."

As if he understood me, Mortiboy let out a long, low meow. Rocky turned around to investigate and the howl was followed up with a hiss. Hudson reached his right hand around behind his seat and stuck his fingers into the grate of the carrier. "Hey, little fella, hang on. We'll be there in a sec." He glanced behind my seat at the cat carrier just as a dirty SUV rounded the corner, coming right toward us.

I yelled. Hudson hit the brakes and pulled the steering wheel to the right. The SUV careened toward us. The Jeep swerved, but not fast enough. The front of the SUV clipped the Jeep. The wheels caught on a snarl of upended tree roots along the side of the road. The Jeep tilted to the left and then fell like a wounded dinosaur. I clutched Rocky to my chest. A cloud of dirt filled the air around us. The SUV backed away from us and drove off.

I undid my seatbelt and climbed out of the car. Rocky crawled across Hudson and hopped in circles in the middle of the road. I grabbed the end of his leash so he couldn't run away and stooped down by Hudson's head.

The heat and dust filled my lungs. I waved my hand through the air to see the damage. Hudson lay very still. A streak of blood ran across his forehead. Seconds after being hit, we were stranded on the side of the road.

# TWO

"Help!" I hollered. "Somebody, help!" I stooped down next to Hudson. "Talk to me," I said. "Say something. Anything."

He opened his eyes and reached his hand out toward me. "I'm okay." He bent down and tried the seatbelt release. It was jammed. "I need you to go to Emma's house and get Jimmy. It's about two hundred feet up the road. He can help." He coughed.

"You couldn't keep the car from tipping. He's not going to be able to lift it."

"He's got a chain on his truck."

I moved Mortiboy's cage to a safe spot by the front wheels of the Jeep. "I don't want to leave you," I said. "What if another car comes along? They aren't going to know you're inside the car. You could get hit—or worse."

"This isn't a busy street. You'll be back before anybody else comes along."

"I'm not taking any chances," I said. I yanked my suitcase out of the back of the Jeep, flipped it open, and pulled out my orange floral bathing suit. I set the suitcase in the middle of the street and knotted the bathing suit to the handle. If nothing else, it would get someone to slow down. I leaned down and kissed Hudson's forehead. "I'm taking Rocky. We'll be back before you realize we left."

Hudson was right about the directions. Around the corner, past several Dracaena plants, was a long driveway. A metallic mint-green convertible sat in front of the garage. I went to the front door and rang the bell. Hudson's sister, Emma, answered.

"Madison! I didn't hear you and Hudson pull up." She started to hug me, but I stopped her with my outstretched hand.

"Is Jimmy here?" I asked.

She looked taken aback. "He's not back from the store."

"I'm sorry to be so brusque, but this is an emergency. Somebody ran us off the road. The Jeep tipped and Hudson is trapped inside."

"Is he hurt?"

"He's okay for now. I'm going back before anybody else drives along that road. It's right up there at that narrow turn. Is there anybody else who can help us?"

"It's just me and Heather." Next to Emma, a small blonde girl stood in a pink T-shirt and jean shorts. Her knees were covered with brush burns that came from tomboyish behavior. Emma turned to the girl. "Heather, keep looking for your bunny. I'm going with Madison."

"What about Rocky?" Heather asked.

"He can stay here with you," I said. Emma reached into a mother-of-pearl bowl next to the door and pulled out a set of keys while I looped Rocky's leash over the metal end of the banister. "I'll be right back," I told him.

Emma pulled the door shut. I ran toward the convertible and jumped in the passenger side. The car roared to life. She backed out of the drive and then drove toward the hairpin turn. When we reached the accident scene, the Jeep was upright and Hudson was sitting on the back, scratching Mortiboy's ears. A man I didn't know sat next to Hudson. The man eased himself down and approached Emma's car.

"Where'd you come from?" Emma asked. She left her giant car parked in the middle of the road and climbed out. I followed suit.

"I wasn't far. Came around that turn and saw a suitcase in the middle of the road. Good thinking," he said to me. "You must be Madison." He approached me and held out his hand. "Jimmy McKenna," he said. "Emma's husband."

"Good thing you came along when you did," I said. "The SUV

that hit us must have known what was going to happen. He took off like he was afraid of getting caught."

Jimmy looked down the road. "It was an SUV? I don't think anybody on this road owns one."

"It wasn't an SUV," Hudson said. "It was a truck. A black truck."

"It was a dirty SUV," I said. "But other than that, I can't tell you very much. It happened so fast and as soon as Hudson hit the brakes, the dirt made a cloud around us."

"Those dirt clouds travel fast. You want to make money fast? Open a car wash in the desert." Jimmy turned to Hudson. "You sure you're okay, man?"

"I'm okay. The Jeep's a little worse for wear though."

"That Jeep has seen more action than that. You sure you don't want to go to the hospital and get looked at?"

"I'm fine," Hudson said. He adopted a slight southern dialect. "I got my girl and my cat. Reckon I don't need much more than that, now do I?"

"I reckon you don't," Jimmy said. "How 'bout you and Madison follow Emma to the house? I'll bring up the rear to make sure you're safe."

I looked back and forth between the two men's faces. If I hadn't known better, I would have thought Hudson and Jimmy were related, not Hudson and Emma. They acted like friends who'd known each other forever. Emma was lucky they got along. I glanced in her direction and smiled, but she didn't notice. She was busy looking down the street behind us. One by one we climbed into our cars and started the short procession back to their house. This time Emma pulled her convertible into the garage, leaving room in the driveway for the Jeep and the truck. Emma opened the door to the house and ran out. I untied Rocky's leash from the bannister. He nipped everybody's ankles and then ran inside, hopping around Hudson's niece, Heather. She squealed and ran inside the house with Rocky on her heels.

It sure wasn't like Monday night around my place.

*   *   *

Hours later, Emma, Jimmy, and I sat around the backyard enjoying dinner on the grill. Heather chased Rocky around the backyard, her long blonde hair flying behind her at the same angle as Rocky's long fur. Past the edge of the property line, a large construction crane was silhouetted against an orange sky. A white sign announced new luxury condos under construction. Hudson, who had picked up a nice layer of dirt from being pinned under the Jeep, had gone directly to the shower when we arrived. He joined the rest of us right about when Jimmy was finishing with the first round of burgers.

"Huds, I'm curious. Did you see the driver of this black truck?" Jimmy asked. I could tell from the look on his face that he was poking friendly fun at us. "Madison here says the driver was a tall redhead with a beard."

"And he had a hook for a hand and a peg leg too," I said, playing along.

"So it was a man," Jimmy said.

"I think so. Hudson, did you see him?"

"Not really," he said. "It happened so fast and it was right after Mortiboy started crying."

"Well, if nobody saw him then there's nothing to report," Emma said. She stood over a line of paper plates that each held an open hamburger bun and a short stack of lettuce, onion, and tomato.

"I still don't like it," Jimmy said. "This is our neighborhood. If somebody is tearing up these streets, then it might be worse the next time." He pulled each patty off the grill and slid it onto a bun. "You know what I need to do? Tomorrow, remind me to put up a sign by that hairpin turn. Can't hurt, right? Remind people to slow down."

"Whoever it was will probably never even come back this way," Emma said. "Now for a more important subject. Who wants ketchup?"

After dinner and a thorough rehashing of Hudson's brush with death, I declared myself a victim of jetlag. The two-hour time difference wasn't extreme, but I was used to getting up between five and six to swim each morning. Coupled with the events of the day and a steady stream of yawns every fifteen minutes, I knew it was time to retire. Emma led me into the house and showed me the layout.

"Sorry to turn into a pumpkin so early," I said. "It's only nine. You would think an adult could handle a two-hour time change."

"It's been a big day for all of us," she said. "I'm glad you were the one to call it a night instead of me."

"Did you find her rabbit?"

"What?"

"Heather's rabbit. She was looking for it when I came to the door."

Emma sighed and shook her head. "I thought Heather forgot about that stuffed rabbit months ago. I haven't seen her with it in ages. But she got it into her head that she wanted him to say hello to you and Hudson when you got here so we've been looking all over this place trying to find it."

I smiled. "She had that rabbit with her the first night I met you two. It's kind of sweet that she wanted him to say hello to us."

"Sweet? Maybe. A pain in the butt now that I have no idea where she put him? Absolutely. I told her to see if she left it next door and that led to the slumber party—small miracle." She tipped her head toward the backyard where the men had stayed behind. "Those two could go on all night and usually I'm the party pooper." She led me down a hallway to a pretty guest bedroom made up in shades of lilac, aqua, and white. Rocky was curled up on the middle of the coverlet next to my tasseled straw hat. My suitcase sat on the floor next to the bed. Hudson's luggage was lined up against the wall. "Hudson knows where we keep everything, but if there's something you need and he doesn't know, don't hesitate to ask." She surprised me with a sisterly hug. "I'm really happy we'll get to spend some time together," she said, and then left.

I took advantage of my alone time to shower and change into peony pink cotton PJs trimmed with white eyelet. I did some light unpacking, mostly to keep the wrinkles from my cotton dresses, and then set up a makeshift corner for Rocky (just in case). I suspected he'd stay exactly where he was, at least until Mortiboy staked the center of the bed out for himself like he did on the occasional nights that Hudson and I watched TV from the comfort of his bedroom.

After hanging up my dresses, I returned to the bathroom to set out my ibuprofen, vitamins, and supplements. A few years back I'd torn the ligaments in my knee, and despite months of physical therapy, I was left with chronic pain. I tried to keep my intake on an as-needed basis, but the plane ride and the heat had done a number on me. I took eight hundred milligrams of the anti-inflammatory and followed with a chewable antacid and calcium supplement.

The only other pills that I'd brought were to help me wind down at the end of the day. My regular doctor had prescribed me a sedative, but relying on drugs to get through the night wasn't a road I wanted to travel. It was also the reason I had yet to stay over at Hudson's house. In so many ways, I felt I could tell Hudson anything, but years of independence had left me protective of what I viewed as my faults. While our relationship had progressed beyond the PG-13 rating, I'd always found a way to politely decline his invitations to spend the night.

"Madison?" Hudson called.

"In here," I answered.

Moments later, I heard him enter the bedroom.

"I don't want to blow our first night of romance, but I have to ask: are you as tired as I am?"

I tucked the bottle of sleeping pills into the bottom of my overnight kit and opened the door. "If it's possible, I might be more tired than you."

"Then our timing is spot on." He turned down the covers on my side. "You okay with the sleeping arrangements?"

"Sure," I said. "Are you?"

He stepped away from the bed and put his arms around me. "Truth? I already knew Emma and Jimmy only had one guest bedroom. The sleeping arrangements were half the reason I took the job."

I wish I could say I fell into a blissful sleep and woke up the next morning. The falling asleep part turned out to be true, but unfortunately for anybody in a five-mile radius, I woke up screaming.

# THREE

"Madison, wake up. I'm right here." Hudson's voice was a new addition to the nightmares. I felt a hand on my arm and I shook it off as if I were fighting off an attacker. "Ow," he said.

The line between my dream and reality widened and I woke up. I was sweaty and the sheets were tangled. Hudson sat next to me, one hand covering his eye, the other hovering by my shoulder.

"Did I hit you?" I asked.

"Not hard." He moved his hand away from his face and I saw a small red welt on his cheek.

"I'm sorry." I pushed the sheets away from my body to cool down. There was a knock on the door. The clock on the nightstand said 3:37.

Hudson stood up and went to the door. Jimmy was on the other side. "Is everything okay in here?"

Even though the question had been directed to Hudson, I answered. "I'm sorry I woke you. I had a nightmare. The accident— and the unfamiliar bed—I think it played tricks with my subconscious. Did I scare you?"

"Don't worry about me. Can I bring you anything? Water? Brandy?"

I thought of the pills in my overnight kit. If I took one now, I'd be back asleep shortly after four. "I'll be fine," I said to both of them. Hudson said something to Jimmy, who nodded and eased the bedroom door shut behind him.

I slipped out of bed and into the bathroom and swallowed a pill. When I returned, Hudson lay on his side, his head propped on his fist. "How long have you been having nightmares?" he asked gently.

"A couple of months. I thought they'd fade, but they haven't. I don't know how to make them stop."

"Time is the only way to control them," he said. He reached out and ran his hand back and forth over my hand. "You need time to heal. What you went through—anybody would have nightmares after that."

"It's been five months."

"You have to be patient." He pulled back the covers and I slid between the sheets. He extended one arm and I nestled against him.

"It's late," I said. "Or early. But I'd like to try to get more sleep before we have to get up." The pill took effect, granting me thick dreamless peace until the sun was up.

The next morning, I found Emma alone in the kitchen. "The boys went on ahead to the job site," she said. "They took Jimmy's truck. Hudson said you're familiar with the Jeep, but if you'd rather not drive it, you can borrow my bike. It's only a couple of miles and it might be fun for Rocky to ride in the basket."

"That does sound like fun," I said. "But I wasn't planning on taking Rocky with me to the job site."

Emma poured me a cup of coffee from a sleek chrome electric pot. We chatted briefly about this and that, the kind of small talk you engage in when there's an elephant in the room and nobody wants to acknowledge it.

Finally, Emma said, "Did something happen last night that I should know about?"

"Nightmare. Remember those abductions in Dallas? You were there visiting Hudson, but you left because he thought it was too dangerous for you to stay." She nodded at the memory. "That's when they started."

She sipped from a white mug lined in pink glaze. "Does

Hudson know about them? He must if you've ever spent the night with him."

"I haven't—we haven't—I mean, we have, but—I told him about the nightmares last night."

She set her mug down and dropped into the chair across from me. "That's a pretty big bombshell for your first full night together."

"Emma, I'm forty-eight years old and my last relationship ended badly. I thought I'd put all of these worries behind me."

"Do you wish you had? You and my brother had a perfectly good working relationship. I know you make him happy, but do you wish things had stayed like that?"

It was a personal question, made even more so because it came from Hudson's sister. Emma had been nothing but friendly to me since I'd first met her, long before Hudson and I changed the nature of our relationship.

Hudson and I had met when he answered my ad for a handyman. The last thing I'd been looking for was a romance, which had been the main reason I'd chosen to only see him as a colleague. Over the course of time, there had been other reasons too. A few of them were still pretty valid. But after a couple of life-threatening experiences over the past few years, I'd come to view my future differently. As in, I chose to have one rather than not.

I added some milk to my coffee and took a sip before answering. "I wish a lot of things had turned out differently, but not Hudson. Everything that happened led me here. Life's too short. That's the main thing I learned from what happened back home. Other than that, wishing doesn't seem to accomplish a whole heck of a lot."

"What about the other guy?" she asked unexpectedly. "The cop?"

A low-level hum rattled my body at the mention of Tex. A year ago, when I thought romance wasn't going to be a factor in my life, I'd discovered an attraction to not one but two men. Because of similar interests and compatibility, Hudson was the one I chose. If I hadn't wanted to talk about the nightmares, then I *really* didn't want to admit that sometimes in my nightmares, Tex was the face of the man I'd killed. I suspected a therapist would have plenty to say about that.

"Tex? I mean, Lieutenant Allen?" She nodded. "What about him?"

"Have you ever talked to him about the nightmares? In his line of work, I imagine he's had to figure out a way to deal with stress. Maybe he'd understand."

I relaxed slightly. "Maybe he would." I didn't add that I hadn't talked to Tex since then. Having made my choice between the two men, it felt somehow wrong to seek out the connection that Tex and I had, like an acknowledgement that there was something missing from my relationship with Hudson. The truth was, Tex was the last person I thought I'd miss, but I did.

The kitchen grew silent as Emma put away the signs of breakfast. I declined her offer of eggs and ate a bowl of cereal instead. When I was finished, I packed a few essentials into a small yellow bag with a synthetic Gerbera daisy affixed to the front and draped it across my lime green short-sleeved top and white pedal pushers printed with pineapples (Butterick 8989). I pulled on a white straw hat with multicolored tassels, slipped my feet into a pair of yellow canvas sneakers, and eased a pair of white-framed sunglasses onto my head.

"Are you sure you don't mind loaning me your bike?"

"Not at all. I bought it years ago and it mostly sits around in the garage. Jimmy will be happy to see it getting some use."

"Where is the job site?" I asked.

"Head like you're going back to the airport. They're working out by the tip of Whitewater River. Here," she said, and pushed a sheet of paper toward me. "Jimmy wrote directions for you."

"I'm beginning to wonder how you managed to stay out of this project."

"The idea of working outside in this temperature is crazy. I don't know how they talked you into it in the first place."

I shrugged. "It sounded like fun," I said.

She put both hands up palm side out. "I wouldn't have said yes, but that's me."

I slipped on my sunglasses, gave Rocky a talk about playing nice with Heather, Mortiboy, and Emma, and left. The bike was a nice change from sitting in a car, but I was particularly cautious thanks to the unfamiliar streets and yesterday's accident. Soon enough, I passed signs announcing Whitewater River. I approached a public lot and swung the bike up to a rack next to a copper statue of a cactus plant. The lot was half full, though I didn't see any people milling about.

In front of me was a sand-covered path that led to a small wooden pier. A map near the copper cactus pictured the entirety of Whitewater River, making it clear that 90 percent of it was to my left. The pier jutted out over a narrow body of water and was empty except for an army-issue duffle bag that sat to the side next to an abandoned Starbucks cup. I walked down the pier and looked around for signs of Hudson or Jimmy or anybody else. As I reached the end, their voices carried across the water to me. I spotted them standing on the other side.

I cupped my hands around my mouth and called out Hudson's name. He looked away from the group, but didn't see me right away. I took my hat off and waved it back and forth over my head. The gesture caught his attention, but not before my hat slipped from my fingers and sailed into the river.

I stooped down below the railing and stretched my arm forward, trying to grab the hat. The current slowly brought it closer to me. When it was within reach, I kept one hand on the wooden rail and tried to grab it.

That's when I saw a pale white face staring up at me from underneath the surface of the water.

# FOUR

I screamed. I scrambled backward on the pier, the soles of my sneakers pushing off against the base of the railing. My hat floated past and continued its journey downstream. My cell phone rang. I pulled it out and answered.

"What happened?" Hudson asked. I looked across the river. Already the group of men had broken up. The bridge was to my left, and commuter traffic was heavy. They would have made better time if they'd had a boat.

"There's a body below the surface of the water," I said. "A man. I'm going to call 911."

"After last night, your mind might be playing tricks on you." He paused. "I'll be right there."

The hesitation in his voice troubled me more than I cared to admit, but the idea that I'd imagined what I saw was worse. I stood up and crept to the edge of the pier and looked into the water a second time. It took several seconds of scanning the surface before I made out the movement of human hair waving gently beneath the surface.

I hadn't imagined it.

"911, please state your name and emergency," said a female voice thick with a Spanish accent.

"My name is Madison Night. I'm at Whitewater River on the pier next to the copper cactus statue. There's a man in the water. I think he's dead. His face is bloated and he's below the surface. He hasn't floated up so I think he's tied to something."

I heard her fingers clicking on a keyboard. "Do you know the identity of this man?" she asked.

"No. I'm from out of town."

"Are you in immediate danger?"

"I don't think so."

"Are you alone?"

"At the moment, yes, but my group is headed this way."

"Where were they?"

"On the other side of the river."

"Please remain where you are, ma'am. I'm sending the police."

I moved from the pier to the base of the cactus statue. If the temperature was high, I didn't notice. I stared out across the parking lot at the scattering of cars, focusing on the bucolic scene and not the memory of the face in the water. By the time I'd taken inventory of the cars in the lot, Hudson and Jimmy's truck pulled in. Hudson jumped out as the sound of sirens filled the air.

"After I hung up, I looked again. I didn't imagine it. There's a man in the water and he's dead."

"Come here," he said. He opened his arms and I stepped into them. "I didn't mean to doubt you."

I rested my head against his black T-shirt and felt myself start to shake. His arms tightened around me. A black and white SUV with "Palm Springs Police" painted on the side in bright blue letters parked next to the Jeep. The officer, a black man in a uniform, climbed out of the driver's side. His partner, a short but compact white man with a shaved head, climbed out of the passenger side. They headed toward me. "Madison Night?" the black officer asked.

I pulled away from Hudson. "That's me."

"Officer Buchanan," he said. "This is Officer Truman." I shook Buchanan's hand first and then Truman's. Buchanan put his hands on his belt, jostling the equipment that hung from it. "Can you show us what you saw?" he asked.

I walked them down the pier toward the spot where I'd seen the body. The sun was approaching its apex, and a bright shimmery glare hit the surface of the water, making it difficult to see into the depth. I pointed. "Right there is where I saw him," I said. "He's under the water. His hair is long enough to float around."

"I don't see anything," Officer Truman said. His mirrored sunglasses made it difficult to tell where he was looking, but I sensed he was looking directly at me.

"I think he's caught on something," I said.

"You think he's caught on something," Officer Buchanan repeated slowly. "Why do you think this, Ms. Night?"

"His head rose up to just below the surface but then disappeared. If he wasn't caught, his whole body would float up, wouldn't it?"

"Are you a doctor? Medical examiner? Do you have experience with dead bodies?"

I didn't think it was the time to acknowledge the answer to one out of his three questions was yes. "I'm a decorator. I'm here from Texas on a job. My team came here earlier today and I was meeting up with them. They were on the other side of the river and I was trying to get their attention by waving my hat. I dropped the hat and it landed in the water. I saw the body when I was trying to get it back."

The two officers looked at each other. I stood back from the end of the pier and pointed to the abandoned duffle bag. "What about that?" I asked. "It was here when I got here. Maybe there's identification inside. Maybe it belongs to the body."

"There is no body," Buchanan said. Truman stooped next to the duffle bag and used a pen to lift one of the handles and look inside.

"There is a body. I saw it."

"Not much we can do until we see it," Buchanan said. "Can you show me again where you saw this body?"

"Over here." I led him back to the railing where I'd waved to Hudson and pointed down into the water. "I know this is an unusual call, but trust me, Officer, I know what I saw."

Hudson and Jimmy approached. Hudson held a long silver pole with a net on the end of it. Jimmy had his hands in his pockets and kept his eyes diverted. He was embarrassed by me. I'd been in his town for less than a day and between the accident, the nightmares, and now this, I'd already been involved in three separate dramas. Any first impressions I might have made would be impossible to overcome.

"I know this isn't standard equipment, but Jimmy had this in the truck and we thought maybe you could send it down in the water. If there's something there, you'll find it. If not, you won't."

"Who are you?" Buchanan asked.

"Hudson James. Jimmy's brother-in-law."

"Do you know this woman?" he asked, and tipped his head toward me.

Hudson nodded. "She's part of our team," he said.

Buchanan looked across our faces. "What kind of team? What are you doing here?"

Jimmy spoke up. "We're a construction crew. I bought the land out by the quarry and we're going to build a strip mall. These two just came in from out of town, so we're meeting today to get them up to speed on the plans and schedules."

Buchanan seemed to accept that as a positive endorsement of my character. He took the pole from Hudson and handed it to Truman. "You want to give it a try?"

"Sure. Might come up with some bass." The two officers laughed.

My stomach turned with the casual way the officers were treating the situation. I knew what they'd find when they put the pole into the water. I turned away from the scene and faced Hudson. "Does anybody mind if I sit in the truck?"

"Just don't leave," Buchanan said.

I left the pier and passed a shiny dark blue Chevy Avalanche with a parking ticket under the windshield wiper. The vehicle was part SUV and part pickup truck. I looked around the rest of the lot and spotted at least six additional SUVs, all of similar body type, all in various states of cleanliness.

My mind was playing tricks on me. It had been a long time

since I'd had a vacation—too long. Part of the reason I'd agreed to this trip with Hudson was because I thought a break from Dallas would be a good thing. I needed to relax and learn to let go of the memories that haunted me.

Hudson joined me. "Want some company?" he asked.

"Please," I said. "I don't think I'm going to be too popular with Jimmy after today."

"He'll get over it."

We sat in the bed of the truck in silence and watched the officers search the area. At first the search was limited to the pier and the water. Soon they were joined by additional vehicles and additional officers, some in uniform, some in wetsuits. Jimmy grew impatient, eventually sending his crew home. Hudson and I remained in the lot. Several hours passed. No body was found.

"I didn't make it up."

"I know you didn't. But without a body, there's not a whole lot they can do." He reached a hand up and stroked my hair. "Do you want to go back to the house? You had a rough night. Maybe we should call it quits."

"No. You said it yourself, I'm part of the team. I came here to work. I don't want Jimmy or anybody else to think that I'm going to be more of a problem than a help."

"Nobody's judging you."

I moved Hudson's hand from my hair and squeezed it. "Not true. *I'm* judging me and right now I don't like the verdict." I smiled. "Give me five minutes to apply a second coat of sunscreen and I'll be good to go."


Eight hours later, after the officers had searched the lakeside grounds and a dive team had searched the river, Officer Buchanan came over and gave us the news. It appeared as though my imagination had cost the city of Palm Springs a bundle of money, and Jimmy had lost an entire day of work. Hudson loaded Emma's bike into the back of Jimmy's truck and we climbed in. As we pulled away from the parking lot, I couldn't help noticing the dark blue Avalanche with the parking ticket was the only vehicle left in the lot.

# FIVE

It was a quiet drive. I stared out the window, wondering if we'd all end up sitting around the grill again, this time talking about my wild story. I doubted it. While last night felt like a bonding evening of shared stories around the adult-version of a campfire, today felt different. Jimmy's attitude toward me had changed from friendly to something more distant. These people didn't know me; they didn't know that it wasn't in my nature to make things up or to seek out the spotlight for dramatic effect. I'd been in their town for all of twenty-four hours and the way he'd see it was that I'd cost him valuable time. First the nightmare and now the face in the water. I'd lost all credibility. Would Tex have believed me? Did it matter?

"Let's go out to dinner tonight," Hudson said.

"Fine with me," I said. "I hope Emma didn't go to any trouble. We should have said something before we left."

"I meant just us." He glanced at me. "After all, this is supposed to be part vacation."

"You mean give Jimmy and Emma the night without us so he can tell her all about what happened today."

"You closed Mad for Mod for a couple of weeks, right?"

"Right. Two-week closure."

"Two weeks is a lot of time to spend together while we're here. I think maybe it's good to establish that it's not going to be the four of us twenty-four seven. We'll be working with Jimmy during the day and sleeping at his and Emma's house at night. You know what they say about fish and visitors. If we don't take the opportunity to go our own way every now and then, it's going to get really tiresome really fast."

Hudson used sound logic to counter my suspicion, but I couldn't shake the feeling that I'd gotten us off on the wrong foot and would have to be conscious of damage control.

"Dinner out sounds nice," I said. "But let's find a place that lets us eat outside, okay? One that has water misters so it doesn't feel so hot and dry. I'd like to take Rocky with us."

"You got it."

Any awkwardness I expected to feel after Jimmy told Emma about the events of the day was avoided by the fact that Emma wasn't home. Jimmy went straight to the kitchen and helped himself to a beer. Mortiboy was on the sofa. He jumped up and walked over to Hudson, who scooped him up and scratched his ears.

Jimmy held up his bottle. "You want one?" he asked Hudson.

"No, Madison and I are going to get cleaned up and go out to dinner. You don't mind, right?"

"Nope. Emma's out shopping for curtains or something. I don't know when she'll be home. If you're going out, I'll order a pizza."

"Where's Heather?" Hudson asked.

"Where's Rocky?" I asked.

Jimmy looked back and forth between us. "Heather was acting up because she couldn't find her stuffed rabbit. The only way to get her to calm down was to let her spend the night at the neighbor's house. Your dog is in your room. I checked on him when I came home."

I excused myself and went to change. Rocky jumped down from the center of the comforter and ran to me, hopping up on his hind legs in his own not-so-subtle quest for attention.

"Hey, Rocky," I said. I eased myself down to the carpet and accepted his puppy kisses. "Do you want to get out of this house tonight?" I asked. "Do you want to go exploring Palm Springs?

Maybe Hudson will take us to Frank Sinatra's house. Or Elvis! Do you want to go see where Elvis used to live? Do you?"

Rocky hopped around and yipped as though seeing where Elvis used to live was the greatest suggestion in the world.

When Hudson told me about the job in Palm Springs, it didn't take me long to accept. Palm Springs was a cornerstone of mid-century design, having the highest concentration per capita in the world. The visitor's center sold maps for five dollars that detailed the residences of famous players from the fifties and sixties. I'd added a few additional sights that I wanted to see to my list and programmed them into my phone's GPS. Our days might be spent working on redeveloping the properties that Jimmy had purchased, but our early mornings and nights would be dedicated to the preserved history, flea markets, and thrift shops around town.

I tucked my hair under a pink-and-white-striped shower cap and hopped under a cool spray to revive myself. I dressed in a soft yellow eyelet dress that was fitted over the bodice and spilled out into a full skirt over flat silver sandals that showed off my lilac pedicure. It had been a splurge prior to leaving, and the technician had talked me into having tiny yellow and white daisies painted onto my toenails. I clipped a pair of vintage daisy earrings onto my ears and freshened up my makeup with a dusting of powder and a fresh coat of sheer pink lip gloss. When I stepped out of the bathroom, Hudson stood in front of me in his jeans and nothing else.

Tempting...

"Wow," he said. "You sure clean up nice."

I adjusted one of the earrings and pointed at the bathroom. "Your turn. Hurry up and we might have time to swing by Elvis's house before we eat." I kept my tone light, hoping that we'd eased past any awkwardness. Jimmy's reception had been lukewarm at best, a far cry from yesterday.

"We've got all the time in the world," he said. He leaned down and kissed me, long and soft and tender and sensual. I put my hands on his naked torso and he drew me close. The kiss lasted long enough to make me forget about dinner. When we pulled apart, he smiled. "Can't keep Elvis waiting," he said. He kissed the tip of my nose and then went into the bathroom.

I packed the map of landmark houses into my handbag and dug a soft yellow leash out of my suitcase. Rocky stood still while I clipped it on and then stood in front of the bedroom door ready to go. I'd thought he'd played with Heather, but maybe he'd been in the bedroom all day. I already wasn't popular with the crew. I wondered what they'd think when I started showing up with my dog.

We arrived at Marrakesh, a Moroccan-themed restaurant, about fifteen minutes after we left the house. The interior of the restaurant was undergoing renovations, but they'd set up small round tents in the parking lot. The tents enclosed semi-circular seating covered in red velvet cushions and small tables with luxurious gold tablecloths. The tent fabric had been pulled together and knotted off with thick gold rope, allowing us a view of the sunset. The opposite side allowed us a view of the empty parking lot. It was a casual restaurant with an elegant vibe. Twinkle lights had been strung in the trees, helping to transform the exterior view.

The three of us approached the hostess station. A pretty brunette in a black shirt and trousers greeted us. She wore a gold nametag that said "Lora" pinned to her shirt.

"We have a reservation for two," Hudson said. The hostess glanced at Rocky. "Okay, for three. The name is Hudson."

She picked up a couple of menus and turned. "Follow me," she said.

Rocky led the way. We were seated at a table for two. The hostess unknotted the cord on the side of the tent and arranged the loosened fabric to give us more privacy.

"I hope you weren't expecting to sit inside," she said. "The builders finished their portion of the interior renovation, but the decorators are running behind schedule. It's going to be amazing when they're done. Are you new to Palm Springs? You need to come back and see it."

"We live in Texas," Hudson said.

She looked at me and made a silly face. "You picked a heck of a time of the year to vacation in Palm Springs. Most of the businesses are closed for the off season. That's why the renovations won't affect our business too much."

"We're out here on a job," I said.

"Madison is a decorator. I bet she'd love to see the inside if you could arrange that," Hudson said. He winked at the hostess, who blushed.

"Sure. Come with me," she said.

Hudson leaned back and stretched his arms across the back of the circular booth. "I'll wait here with Rock. You go get inspired."

I smiled to myself. I'd named my dog after Rock Hudson, but soon after adopting him, "Rock" had morphed into "Rocky." Most of the men I knew continued to call him Rock. I suspected it was a show of masculine solidarity.

I slid over the red velvet cushion and out of the tent, and then followed the hostess inside. "Wow," I said.

"I know, right?" she said in a manner that, to my Pennsylvania-turned-Texas ear, sounded very Californian.

The interior walls of the restaurant were painted in a metallic turquoise. At four-foot intervals, thick purple velvet drapes hung from the ceiling to the floor. They were pulled together and knotted with gold cord similar to what had been used on the tents out front. Low tables covered in gold tablecloths were scattered around the interior. Bench seating, so close to the ground that it appeared to hover, sat on either side of the tables. Rich tapestry fabric in shades of silver, gold, purple, and turquoise had been used to cover the cushions.

"It's amazing," I said in awe. "I have no idea if this is what it looks like in Morocco, but I don't even think I care. If we lived here, I'd want to visit every single night."

"If the owners have anything to say about it, when we reopen there'll be a waiting list for reservations. You're actually pretty lucky. The kitchen is working on a couple of new items and you might get to be a taste tester. Good thing you guys made reservations. It's usually pretty quiet in Palm Springs in September, but there's a business convention in town. They're coming in about an hour and they reserved the rest of the tents."

I wandered closer to the wall and studied the paint, and then ran the velvet wall panels between my fingers. "Maybe I'll do a Moroccan room someday."

"You should." She led me back to the exit and to our tent. "Sorry I couldn't give you more time, but I think my boss was starting to wonder what you were doing." She set down the menus. "It might be a second before your server comes over. Can I get you started with something to drink?"

I ordered a glass of Sauvignon Blanc and Hudson ordered a Hefeweizen. Neither one of us said a word until after she'd returned with both of our drinks and a bowl of water for Rocky.

"This is nice, isn't it? Just you and me."

"You made reservations after what happened today, didn't you? Jimmy was annoyed and you thought it was best for us to do our own thing."

"I thought it would be nice to take you out. Make this more about us than about the job."

"When did you call the restaurant?"

"This afternoon."

"After—"

"Madison, last night you woke up screaming. I thought maybe you and I should talk about it."

I took a sip of my wine and followed it with a gulp of water. I wasn't used to confiding in someone else, but if Hudson and I were going to have any kind of relationship, I needed to let him know what was going on with me. As if he understood my need for support, Rocky wound himself around the leg of my chair and laid down next to my foot.

Sleep hadn't come easy for me since the night five months ago when I'd committed vehicular manslaughter. My hometown had been terrorized by a police impersonator, and I'd been in the wrong place at the wrong time. Surveillance footage had been pulled from the convenience store, and there was enough on that tape to clear me.

It wasn't fear of the repercussions that kept me awake at night. It was the memory of having killed a man. Now, I suffered from horrible nightmares, reliving the experience with varying outcomes.

"I've been having nightmares ever since April. I saw a doctor about it. He says it's a classic sign of post-traumatic stress disorder. He recommended I talk to a psychologist and he gave me a prescription for sleeping pills. I didn't want to take one last night."

"Why not?"

"Being in an unfamiliar bed, in an unfamiliar house, I was afraid to completely relax."

"I don't want you to be afraid to relax around me," he said. "We're going to have to work on that."

"You can't erase bad memories."

"No, but I can help to make good ones."

I'd gotten too close to the impersonator case for a multitude of reasons and had almost ended up a victim myself. Add to that a newfound distrust of authority figures and an overwhelming desire to latch on to someone or something, and you found me in completely unfamiliar territory. The illusion of my formerly valued independent lifestyle had been shattered.

My kneejerk reaction was to keep myself busy so I wouldn't think about what had happened. I gave up the role of landlord and listed my apartment building for sale. Hudson, who had repeatedly declined my offers of partnership in Mad for Mod, had bought the building. And while I'd volunteered to help him restore it to its former 1957 glory, he declined that offer too.

I picked up with business at Mad for Mod and moved into a house that I'd inherited. Drive-bys of the apartment building showed me that he'd torn out the carpets and replaced the light fixtures. As much as I wanted to see what he was doing the place, I needed distance from the building that held so many bad memories, so my skeleton key went unused.

"What does Tex have to say about this?"

I looked up from the table at him. "Why would you ask that?"

"He was as involved as you were. In a different way, but he was. He probably has to deal with this all the time." He reached across the table and put his hand on top of mine. "I know you two are friends. I just assumed—"

"I haven't talked to Tex since we—since then."

"I never asked you to cut him out of your life."

"I know." I pulled my hand away from his and dropped it into my lap. "It's complicated."

Hudson pulled his own hand back and took another pull on his beer. When he set his beer down, he looked at me with concern. "Maybe you should talk to a professional. It might help."

After a dinner of Moroccan chicken and saffron couscous and complimentary samples of red onion confit and fig tarts with cardamom orange cream sauce, we drove around Palm Springs admiring the architecture, the plant life, and the sense of color. We agreed that any formal sight-seeing should wait until daylight hours. Even Rocky seemed to accept the fact that Elvis's house wasn't going to happen tonight.

We drove back to Jimmy and Emma's house, tucked away on a side street a few blocks behind the main road of Palm Springs. I was oddly thankful that last night's interrupted sleep had left me looking forward to sleep tonight. Having told Hudson what was going on felt like a giant weight had been lifted. I braced myself for the inevitable tension that would come from seeing Jimmy again. But as we pulled into the driveway, the shouting that spilled out from inside the house erased everything. Hudson was halfway to the front door when we heard a crash.

# SIX

The front door flew open before Hudson reached it and Jimmy stormed out. Hudson grabbed his upper arm, but Jimmy shook off Hudson's grip. Jimmy yanked the door to his truck open, slammed it shut, and backed out of the driveway at a dangerous speed. The truck spun backward in a semicircle and then took off down the road.

Hudson was in the living room with Emma when I went inside. His arms were around her and she sobbed into his shirt. It sounded to me like she was trying to say something, but her erratic breathing made her words unintelligible. I carried Rocky to the bedroom and told him to behave, and then shut the door behind me.

I went to the kitchen and discovered the source of the crash we'd heard outside. A large clay pot lay broken in the middle of the kitchen floor, surrounded by scattered dirt and an assortment of succulents that had been uprooted. I collected the broken pieces of pottery and set them in the trash, and then found a dustpan and broom next to the refrigerator. I repotted as many of the small succulents as I could in bowls I found under the sink and left them on the counter.

When I finished, I filled a glass with water from a plastic jug in the fridge and carried it out front. Emma sat on the sofa. Hudson sat in the chair adjacent to her.

"Has he ever hurt you?" Hudson asked.

"No—never. We argue, but that's all."

"For how long?"

"Off and on for a year," she said. She looked up at me, and I held the glass of water out. "Thank you," she said. She sipped it and then held it between both hands. "I never know what's going to set him off. I thought—I hoped having the two of you here would make things easier."

"What was the problem tonight?" Hudson asked.

Emma glanced up at me a second time.

"It was me, wasn't it?" I said. "It was what happened today at the river."

"He said you cost them a full day's work. I told him if you thought you saw a body, then you had an obligation to report it. He was mad that I took your side. He said I'm always on the other person's side and never his." She started to cry again.

I put my hand on Hudson's shoulder. His muscles were tense. I'd only seen Hudson truly angry on a few occasions, but I suspected this would be one of them. Regardless of the friendship in place between him and Jimmy, Emma was his sister. She and Heather were the only family he had.

"I'm going to leave you two alone," I said quietly. "Rocky and I will be in the bedroom."

"Madison, wait," Emma said. She brushed the tears from her face. "Can I talk to you for a minute?"

Hudson put his hand on top of mine and then stood up. "I'll take Rock out one last time," he said. He went into the hallway and returned with Rocky hooked to his leash. Neither Emma nor I spoke until the door closed behind him.

I ignored the empty chair and sat on the sofa next to her. I put my hand on her back and rubbed up and down in a comforting manner. "You don't have to talk if you don't want to," I said. "We can just sit here."

"I need to talk to somebody," she said. "But not Hudson. And I can't take a chance that he'll overhear us." She sniffled a few times, her breath still catching occasionally as her lungs caught up with her.

The front door opened and we both looked up. Hudson bent

down and let Rocky off his leash. Rocky bounded over to us, but Hudson remained in the hallway. I tipped my head toward Emma's. "How about tomorrow morning? I was planning on getting up early for a swim before the day got started. Do you want to join me?"

She nodded. We said goodnight and I joined Hudson in the bedroom. He stood on his side of the bed. Tonight it was Mortiboy who took up the space smack in the middle of the comforter.

"This whole trip was a mistake," he said. "Our first getaway should have been a getaway. Not a job, not under somebody else's roof. You're dealing with issues. My sister and her husband are at war." Rocky jumped up onto the bed and Mortiboy hissed at him and swatted his nose. Rocky turned tail and jumped back down on the floor. "Hell, our animals can't even get along."

"If this is anybody's fault, it's mine," I said. "You heard your sister. Jimmy was mad because of what happened at the job site today."

"Emma was right. If you thought you saw a body in the water, then you had an obligation to notify the police."

"Do you believe me?" I asked.

"I believe you because I know you. As morbid as it sounds, I wish there *had* been a body. None of this would have happened."

"There *was* a body. I don't know what happened to it, but it was there." I pulled my pajamas out from underneath my pillow. "I think it might be a good idea for me to swim tomorrow morning. My knee's been pretty swollen since the flight, and it might be wise to do something familiar, try to find a routine while we're here. I told Emma she could come with me if she wanted. Are you okay with that?"

"Sure. It might do her good to get out of the house. I'll stay here and have breakfast ready. When Jimmy comes back, we'll need to clear the air if we expect to work together."


Our plans were for naught. Neither Jimmy nor Emma were home when I woke up the next morning.

Hudson left messages on both of their phones. I cleaned Mortiboy's litter box and took Rocky outside. He ran to the neighbor's house and peed on a low shrub by the corner. Giggling spilled out from inside the house and then two girls' faces appeared in the window. "Rocky came to visit!" Heather said through the screen of the house next door. "Come on!"

I called Rocky back to me, but as soon as the front door opened, he took off for the girls. A woman in an oversized 49ers T-shirt and leggings came out after them. "Girls! Keep it down. It's six o'clock in the morning!"

I walked over and introduced myself. "Hi, I'm Madison Night. I'm staying with Emma and Jimmy for a little while." I pointed to Rocky. "I'm afraid he's to be blamed for your wake-up call. He's mine."

"Don't worry. He didn't wake me up. When you host a slumber party for nine-year-old girls, you sacrifice your sleep. I was hoping to get in some Pilates before they woke up, but I should have known better." She wiped her hands on her shirt and then held one out. "Jo Conway. Nice to meet you."

I shook her hand. "How long was Heather expected to stay?"

"That's the beauty of a sleepover at the neighbor's house. We never really set things in stone. The school bus comes at eight thirty, but I was going to drop Gina off on my way to work. If Emma's too busy, I can take Heather too."

I didn't think it prudent to mention the fight or the fact that both parents were gone this morning, but I also wasn't prepared to take care of a stranger's daughter in an unfamiliar town. "I can't speak for Emma, but I think the girls would enjoy the extra time here to play with Rocky."

"Rocky? Like the Sylvester Stallone movies?"

"Like Rock Hudson." I smiled. "The Y came later. There are some who would say that I was born in the wrong decade."

She smiled and took in my turquoise, yellow, and tangerine vertical-striped top with the zig-zag hem and white cotton shorts (Simplicity 5439). "What do you do for a living?"

"I own a decorating business that specializes in mid-century modern design."

She laughed. "Sounds to me like you know exactly who you are."

"I've had plenty of crises, but crisis of identity hasn't been one of them."

"Divorce?" she asked.

"Nope, never married."

"Lucky. The best thing about mine was the free healthcare." I must have looked confused, because she laughed. "I was married to a doctor," she said.

I heard the door behind me and turned around. Hudson met me with a mug of coffee. "I thought you got lost," he said. He put his hand around my waist. "You're Jo, right?"

"Yep. How'd you know?"

"Emma's my sister. She mentioned somebody with a girl Heather's age bought the place next door. I'm Hudson."

"Nice to meet you."

I turned to Hudson. "Jo volunteered to take the girls to school today. Do you think Emma would be okay with that?"

"I don't see why not."

I looked down at Rocky. I'd already been thinking that taking him with us to a job site with broken and rusted fixtures was a bad idea, more for his safety than any other reason.

"What about Rocky?" I asked Hudson.

Jo answered, "Leave him here with the girls. I'll drop him off with Emma before we leave for the school."

He looked at Jo. "Thanks. I'll let my sister know."

Neither Hudson nor I mentioned that Emma wasn't at the house. It seemed alarmist to wonder when we'd see her again, especially since technically we were her guests. More likely than not, she'd pull into the driveway while we were chatting with her neighbor. I turned and looked toward the road, hopeful. No cars appeared.

*   *   *

The parking lot by the Whitewater River was less full today than yesterday. I credited the early hour. The work team wasn't expected to arrive for over an hour, but neither Hudson nor I were the type to sit around watching a ticking clock.

We parked near the cactus statue. The dark blue Chevy truck was still parked in the same space. A second parking ticket was pinned under the windshield wiper. A light coating of dirt had accumulated over the paint, making the color appear more of a dingy gray-black. While it blended in with the setting, it wasn't a particularly popular color in mid-century decorating.

"Tell me a little more about this project," I asked. "You gave me the highlights, but not the specifics. Why are we at a river?"

"Jimmy has been buying up defunct storefronts and properties that he learned about on a prior job. Some of them are rundown relics of the sixties, some of them are patches of land that for one reason or another came up for sale. He didn't have a plan at first, just thought it would be an investment."

"Has he partnered with a developer?"

"No, this is his own project from start to finish. He financed it himself and has worked out the details. Last year he discovered a whole dump site of partially torn-down buildings from the Salton Sea. You know where that is?"

"Southeast of here, isn't it? At one point it was considered to be the next Palm Springs, right?"

"Yes, but it never got off the ground. Sonny Bono took a special interest in it when he was mayor of Palm Springs, but when he died, his plans died with him. It's a pretty dangerous area now. Street gangs, meth labs, not a pretty place. Not much left from back when it had so much promise. A couple of the buildings—gas stations, coffee shops, dry cleaners, small mom and pop stores—were bulldozed and the rubble was discarded at a local quarry. When Jimmy saw that, he got the idea to bring those architectural elements to his properties in Palm Springs and to create a pocket of businesses with the authentic look of Palm Springs but with modernized services."

"Using existing architecture instead of building new. That's a great idea," I said. We strolled side by side to the end of the pier. Despite our pleasant conversation, I couldn't shake the fact that just yesterday I'd stood in this very same spot and had seen a body floating under the surface. I scanned the river, looking for signs that I hadn't imagined it. Water lapped at the base of the pier, and the water sparkled from the rays of the sun.

We stood there together, letting the sounds of crickets chirping and the faint sound of music from an indeterminate location replace our conversation. Hudson rested his forearms on the railing. I turned my back on the water and leaned against the rail.

After an extended moment of silence, Hudson spoke. "It's nice out here," he said. "Peaceful."

"It almost makes you think I imagined it."

"I wasn't implying that."

"I know, but let's face facts. The police searched high and low and didn't find any evidence of a body. You and Jimmy were here way before me and you didn't see anything either. I guess I've been under more stress than I thought." I kicked the toe of my sneaker against the wooden slats. "Too bad I lost my favorite hat."

"Maybe somebody will find it and turn it in to Lost and Found."

I laughed. "Where exactly would Lost and Found be? There's nobody here."

"Somebody must patrol the area," Hudson said.

A white pickup truck pulled into the lot and parked next to the Jeep. I hadn't been looking forward to seeing Jimmy this morning.

"This is going to be awkward," I said.

Hudson stepped away from the railing and shielded his eyes. "Give me a couple of minutes to talk to him before we get started."

"Sure."

Hudson walked down the length of the pier and crossed the grass toward the parking lot. He was over six feet tall and maintained his lean physique not through working out, but through the physicality of working with carpentry tools and raw materials. Even in the hundred-degree temperature he was dressed in a black T-shirt and jeans. A red and white bandana jutted out of his back pocket, and I suspected that it would be tied around his head within the hour. His black hair had grown out from the Mohawk that he'd had a few months ago, but with his long sideburns, he still looked like he'd taken style tips from Johnny Cash. I didn't know a lot of men who could go full-on man-in-black, but somehow Hudson made the look his own.

I shielded my eyes and watched the two men talk. Their body language appeared cautious, a measure of space between them. Nervous energy kept my yellow sneaker bouncing against the wooden pier. I half expected one of them to throw a punch.

A rattling sound below my foot tore my attention away from the two men. I looked down and saw a set of keys barely jutting out from between the slats. Hudson must have dropped them when we walked up. I bent down and tried to pick them up. No luck. They were wedged between the wood. My knee was too swollen to allow me to squat so I sat down on the wood and stretched my legs out in front of me in a V with the keys in the center. I pulled a six-inch wooden ruler out of my bag and slid it into the space between two slats, and then slowly angled it upward against the bottom of the keys. With steady pressure, they shifted enough for me to get them loose. They were attached to a fob with a Chevy logo. I aimed the thick black remote at the parking lot and pressed the alarm button. The alarm on the abandoned Avalanche tore through the air.

# SEVEN

Hudson and Jimmy looked at me. I hit the unlock button and the alarm ceased. I grabbed the railing and pulled myself up, and then shoved the keys into my small bag. Maybe the police hadn't found a body in the water, but that didn't mean something bad hadn't happened in this very spot. The duffle bag, the spilled coffee cup, the keys wedged between the slats of the pier, and the abandoned vehicle all spoke to the fact that something had gone down here. I looked at the Avalanche again, and again I was struck by the sense that it was the same car that had caused the Jeep to tip. There was nothing tangible to prove I was right. On the contrary, the SUV was spotless. The dirt cloud we'd kicked up would have left it dirty, but it wasn't. Yet something about it niggled at my mind and left me cold despite the warm temperature.

I left the pier and approached the two men. Hudson stepped forward. "What was that alarm?"

"I found some keys on the pier and was checking to see if they belonged to one of us. The owner's probably wandering around somewhere. Sorry if I disturbed your brainstorming session."

Jimmy spoke up. "Madison, I owe you an apology. Last night, the fight you guys heard, that was my fault. I'm not going to make up excuses—I was out of line."

"That's between you and Emma," I said. The timing of our visit seemed to be particularly poor, but I reminded myself this had never been intended to be a social visit. "From what I understood, Hudson and I were asked out here to help with a job. Maybe it's best if we concentrate on that for now."

"Sounds fair. I gave the rest of my crew the day off. Thought maybe it would be best for us to come up with a game plan, lay everything out, and break it down into a timeline. The city approved permits for the next three months, but I don't expect you guys to be here that long. I'd like to use our time to flesh out the schedule. Nobody wants this job to go on indefinitely."

"Works for me," Hudson said.

Jimmy reached into the bed of the truck and pulled out a couple of white rolls of paper that were secured with a rubber band. "It's going to get pretty hot pretty fast. Let's set up under the pavilion."

The two of them led the way. I stayed behind, pretending to look in the truck bed for something else to carry. When I was comfortable they weren't keeping track of my actions, I walked around the front of the Avalanche. The bumper on the front passenger side was slightly dented. I went to the back and took a picture of the plates and caught up with the men.

"Jimmy, I owe you an apology too," I said. He looked at Hudson, who shrugged. He looked back at me. "I cost you some work yesterday. I own my own business, so I understand how a couple of hours at the beginning of a project can put you behind schedule."

"If we're productive today, we can make up time."

"Here's another idea. I never had a chance to see the job site yesterday, so I don't know how much help I'll be today. Hudson told me what the concept was, but why don't you two work here while I take the Jeep and survey the site? I'm a visual person. I haven't seen the buildings you're planning on renovating or the various building components you rescued from the quarry. I'm never going to be the heavy lifter on your team, but if you let me in on the design aspect, you won't regret it."

"She's right," Hudson said. "You won't find anybody who can channel mid-century modern better than Madison. That's why I invited her." He looked at me and winked.

"Okay, sure," Jimmy said. He pulled a small notebook out of

the back pocket of his jeans and scribbled a couple of lines on it. "You should go to the quarry first. Most of what I've accumulated is in bad shape, some of it cosmetic, some of it structural. I expect when we're done with the first wave, we'll have five renovated properties ready to open. That's what I need you guys for. Get those five into shape so I can find tenants. Once the early properties are rented, I'll know how long it takes and I can move on to phase two."

I took the piece of paper. Hudson handed me the keys. I averted my eyes from his. Everything I'd said had been true, but nobody needed to know I had another item on my own agenda. I left them working under the pavilion and drove the Jeep to the police station.

The Palm Springs Police Department was housed in a long red-brick structure with a thick concrete-slab roof. On the exterior wall the words "Palm Springs Police" hung in clean, modern lettering. The grounds outside were manicured and displayed the greenest grass I'd seen since arriving.

I went inside and approached the desk sergeant. "Officers Buchanan and Truman don't happen to be working today, do they?"

"I think Buchanan is in his office. Hold on." He picked up the handset and pressed a few buttons on the phone. "Doris Day's here to see you," he said. Though accurate, the nickname told me I'd already earned a reputation among the local law enforcement.

A few seconds later, Officer Buchanan came out from the back. "Hello, Officer," I said. If I'd been expecting sarcasm or a joke about my appearance, I would have been let down.

"Ms. Night," he said. "What can I do for you?"

"I wanted to follow up on yesterday."

"Ms. Night, it's okay. There's no need to come out here to apologize for calling us."

I pulled the set of keys out of my handbag. "I found these at the park this morning."

He stared at the keys but didn't take them. "Somebody lost

their keys. You probably want to take them to Parks and Recreation's Lost and Found."

"They were jammed between the slats on the pier. I almost didn't see them," I said. "They were probably underneath the duffel bag you saw yesterday."

"Could be," he said.

He tucked his thumbs into his pockets and let his fingers dangle down in front. It was the same way Tex stood, and I briefly wondered if they taught a class on male intimidation body language in police academies across the country.

I set the keys on the counter. "There's a dark blue Chevy Avalanche in the parking lot. It was there yesterday as well. The tag on those keys matches the license plate on it. The car has a couple of parking tickets tucked under the windshield, like it's been sitting there for a few days."

"Maybe the driver can't move his car because he lost his keys. All the more reason for you to take them to Lost and Found."

"Or maybe the car owner is the body I saw in the water yesterday."

Officer Buchanan adjusted his stance slightly and cocked his head to the side. "Ms. Night, we did a thorough, by-the-book search of the park after you called us. Spent a lot of taxpayer money by getting a dive team to search the river too." He crossed his arms over his chest. "When I came back to the station yesterday, I did a little digging around. Turns out there was a little more involved in what happened than I initially knew."

"So you found something. Good." I pulled my phone out. "I took a picture of the license plate on the Avalanche. You could run it and see who owns it, maybe start to get some answers."

"I ran a background check on you. Standard procedure for when somebody reports a crime—especially when we can't find the crime they're reporting. Do you know what I found out?"

I stood very still. I became aware of the lack of circulation in the small police station, the prickly heat of the desert temperature causing me to sweat under my arms and down my back.

"This isn't your first brush with the police, is it, Ms. Night?"

"I am a law-abiding citizen," I said with more conviction than I felt. "I don't know who you talked to, but if any of them said otherwise, I want to know names."

"We heard about those abductions in Dallas," he continued. "Hell of a case. Your involvement would have shaken up anybody. Have you gotten any counseling?"

"What happened in Dallas has no bearing on the body I saw in the water." I picked up the keys. "These keys are a clue, just like the duffel bag and the empty coffee cup were clues. And the abandoned SUV in the parking lot is a clue. Why are you refusing to listen to me?" I looked around. Buchanan had been joined by Truman and another officer, who stood at the back of a hallway. I hadn't realized how much my voice had risen until I stopped talking. My throat constricted and I willed myself to calm down and get control. "Yes, I've been having a hard time dealing with what happened in Dallas. I think anybody would."

Buchanan held his hand up. "Being responsible for the death of a person is not to be taken lightly. First time I shot someone I had to take six months off the force to get a grip. If you ignore what happened, you're going to be plagued by flashbacks. Your mind will invent things that aren't there." He paused slightly, long enough for me to recognize he wasn't talking about his own experience—he was telling me what I thought I'd seen yesterday had been a manifestation of my suppressed memories. "Pretty soon you'll have trouble sleeping, and then you'll have trouble getting along with the very same people you always got along with. Does any of this sound familiar?"

I didn't say anything. I didn't have to.

"Don't let this disrupt your life, Ms. Night."

He'd hit too many nails on the head for me to discount what he said, the most important being his closing words of advice. I put aside my pride. "I don't know how long I'm going to be in Palm Springs. Can you recommend anybody?"

He nodded twice and stepped behind the front desk. He wrote

a name on a sheet of paper and handed it to me. "Call Albert Hall. He's the doctor I talked to when I needed counseling. Not sure if he's accepting new patients. Tell him I referred you."

"Thank you," I said. I folded the paper and slid it into my small wicker bag.

"I hesitate to tell you this, but I don't want you to get the wrong idea. That phone call I made to the Lakewood Police Department...well, I may have made it sound like you were a troublemaker, and they set me straight pretty quickly. Seems the police captain is quite a fan."

"Captain Washington and I got to know each other over the case last April."

"Captain Washington retired last week. I'm talking about his replacement."

"He retired?" I asked. Seemed like the case had impacted just about everybody who'd been connected to it.

"I'm surprised you didn't know. One of his lieutenants got the job. Told me to call him Tex."

# EIGHT

*Tex*

So Madison Night was out of town. On one hand, it was good to know. He'd stop watching out for her little blue Alfa Romeo on the streets of Lakewood. On the other hand, she probably hadn't gone to Palm Springs alone. She was living her life and he was living his. They were two entirely different people from entirely different worlds. It was for the best.

This bit about seeing a body in the water was troubling though. Madison had been in the middle of more than one of Tex's investigations and she'd shown a knack for seeing things others often did not. His first impression of her had been so far off base he'd questioned whether or not he was losing his edge. But after getting to know her, he recognized what made her different. She valued her independence to a level that went beyond a desire for equality. She'd experienced painful loss and betrayal in her life before they'd met and it had left her unapologetic about who she was and unafraid in a way he didn't expect.

He'd lost count of how many times he picked up the phone to talk to her. Especially after Captain Washington announced his retirement. It wasn't like Tex had been pining away for a desk job, but things had changed after the abductions. He'd been on the verge of going renegade to try to get justice. Twenty-five years on the force and he'd never come close to crossing that line before. He scared himself with his capacity for anger and his need to right things. If it hadn't been for Madison's involvement, the case might have had a very different outcome.

Tex picked up the phone and called Madison's design studio. The message told him her business was closed for two weeks. They'd both turned the page on their respective lives. There was no point in leaving a message.

# NINE

So in the wake of the Lakewood abductor case, Captain Washington had retired and Tex had been promoted. I should have been happy for Tex. I couldn't blame him for not telling me. I'd been the one to retreat from whatever odd friendship we'd formed over the past two years, but finding out like this hurt.

I tried to hide my reaction. "Oh, you mean Lieutenant Allen."

"Captain Allen now," Buchanan said. "He told me you might not know about his promotion. Like I said, he spoke pretty highly of you. Said it was no accident you ended up involved in that case and you went out on a limb for the precinct. He also said he's been worried about you." He pointed to my handbag. "Do yourself a favor. Try to get an appointment with Dr. Hall."

I smiled and thanked him, and then left the police station. I sat in the Jeep and stared at the number written on the piece of paper for two solid minutes before pulling out my phone and making the call.

When a recording answered, I hesitated for only a moment. "Dr. Hall, my name is Madison Night. I'm staying in Palm Springs for a couple of weeks, and your number was given to me by Officer Buchanan at the police department to help me work through a few issues. Please let me know if you're accepting new patients and if we can set up an appointment." I said my phone number, repeated it for courtesy, and hung up.

I headed back toward the park. If the police were right and the keys belonged to someone who needed them to drive their car away, then I was making a stranger's life more difficult by holding onto them. I turned off the main road and followed a series of hand-painted signs indicating Parks and Recreation. About a mile down a dirt trail, I skidded to a halt next to a small wooden cabin with a sign out front that said, "Office." I parked the Jeep and approached the building.

Like just about everything else, the windows had a layer of dirt on them. I tried to look inside, but couldn't see through the glass. I wiped my hand across the outside of the window, leaving a small smudged circle, and pressed my face up to the glass again.

"Can I help you?" said a voice from behind me.

I stood up straight and turned. A woman in a khaki shirt and Bermuda shorts stood in front of me. She had a patch over the left sleeve that said "City of Palm Springs, California," in a circle around an orange and yellow image of palm trees. Embroidered on a patch above her left chest pocket was the name Lora. It took me a moment to realize why she looked familiar.

"You work at the Moroccan restaurant, don't you? I ate there last night. I'm the decorator."

"I thought I recognized you."

"You work here too?"

"Yep. It's the curse of Palm Springs in the off season. Everybody cuts back their hours so a lot of us work two jobs to pay the bills." She smiled. "I'm Lora," she said, pointing to her shirt.

"Madison," I said. I glanced down at my striped top as if looking for a name tag, but then looked back up and smiled.

"Let me guess. You're looking for the restrooms? They're over there." She pointed to a building off to the side of us.

"I'm not here for the restrooms. You, um, you didn't happen to find a straw hat with multicolored tassels on it, did you?"

"Nope, sorry. When did you lose it?"

"Yesterday."

"Give it a couple of days. It might turn up."

I pulled the keys out of my bag. "I also wanted to turn these in to Lost and Found. I found them on the pier on Whitewater River. They were jammed between the slats. There's an abandoned SUV in the parking lot, and I think whoever drives it might be looking for them."

She took the keys and stared at them for a few seconds. The angle of the sun highlighted the planes of her face. "What makes you think the car's abandoned?" she asked.

"It's been there for a few days."

She shifted her attention from the keys to me. "You've been keeping track?"

I smiled. "Not intentionally. I noticed the car yesterday when I was first at the river and again today. When I told the police about the keys, they suggested the owner might have lost them and I should bring them to you."

"How'd the police get involved?" The rhythm of her voice was different. I studied her face, trying to place what it was that had changed. When I'd first arrived, she'd seemed casual, relaxed. It could have been in my head, like everything else, but I sensed she was making an effort to appear calm while hiding other emotions below the surface.

"I thought I saw something in the river yesterday and I called the police. Turned out to be my imagination."

I expected her to press me for more information, but she seemed satisfied with my answer as is. She looked back down at the keys in her hand and rubbed her thumb back and forth over the Chevy logo. "I'll put these in lost and found, but if the car's been there for a few days and the keys were on the pier, it doesn't sound to me like the owner looked very hard."

"How long do you hold on to lost items?"

"Thirty days."

"What happens to them when nobody picks them up?"

"You don't think the owner is going to come looking for them, do you?"

"It was just a question."

Her fist closed around the keys. "We say thirty days, but we usually don't throw things out until the bin gets full. Sometimes the finder calls us to see if an item was claimed and if not, they make a case for finder's keepers. Not sure that applies in this case," she finished.

While we were talking, a man wandered into the park. He was tall and thin, dressed in a torn T-shirt and faded camouflage pants that were frayed at the hems. His face was gaunt with pronounced cheekbones and an upturned nose. His thinning black hair was combed straight back, exposing a high forehead. I hadn't seen a car drive up and wasn't sure where he'd come from.

Lora looked at him and shook her head, as if telling him to go away. Her eyes cut to me and then back to him.

"How long until somebody runs the plates on the car?" I asked. "It's just sitting there collecting tickets."

"Towing a car costs the city too much money. Since we're in the off season, it's cheaper to leave it where it is. They won't tow until after it's been there for at least a week, maybe longer." She put the key into her pocket. "Problems like this tend to solve themselves. I'm sure the owner will come around."

I didn't say anything to Lora, but I could think of one type of person who wouldn't come around to collect their car: a dead one.

Too many thoughts were crowding my mind: the body in the water, the abandoned SUV and the recovered keys, and now Lora. The only thing for me to do was the one thing I'd done in the past: throw myself into work.

I followed Jimmy's directions to the quarry and parked in an expanse of loose rubble that resembled a parking area. I climbed out of the Jeep, sprayed my face, arms, and ankles with a misting of sport-level sweat-proof sunscreen, and approached the dumpsite.

Hudson hadn't been kidding about what Jimmy had accumulated. If I'd originally had any doubt about the potential of taking a strip of vacant and rundown businesses and converting them into a mid-century enclave, I had more than enough evidence in front of me to put those doubts at ease. The quarry, easily two hundred feet wide and fifty feet deep, was filled with signs and architectural elements from businesses established fifty years earlier. The sun had bleached them to washed-out pastels, but hours of sanding and repainting would restore them to their glorious bright colors, perfectly perfect for the desert.

The perimeter of the quarry gave me a good view of the wreckage that had been amassed in the center of it below. There were metal arrows and zig zag archways, beams and poles that would set off entrances. Giant letters piped in now-broken neon tubes were mounted on pastel rectangles, spelling out LIQUOR. One façade appeared to have been dumped there almost completely intact. The lettering along the roofline simply said, "Dot's Kitty Cat Lounge."

It gave me an idea.

I went back to the Jeep and rummaged around the back until I found my sketchpad and markers. I stuffed as many markers into my small handbag as I could, and then scanned the perimeter of the quarry until I located a narrow set of stairs that led down to the bottom. Minutes later, I stood among the cast off relics, pausing every now and then to stop and sketch.

I assumed it had been Jimmy and his crew who moved the discarded fixtures to the landfill, because up close, I could tell they'd been placed with a modicum of care. Narrow spaces between each set of building scraps allowed me to weave between them, knocking on and climbing over the individual pieces. After an indulgent stroll around everything and a makeshift inventory in my notebook, I balanced on a once-red now-pink metal arrow that pointed to a yellow circle with faded letters.

I flipped to a blank page in my notebook. Jimmy would have no problem finding the decorative elements to add to whatever business he wanted to rent out to, but what if he approached it differently? What if, instead of renting out and then retrofitting, he determined what businesses he'd want in his small pocket of Palm Springs and then offered incentives toward new business owners to set up shop there? Palm Springs already had an assortment of great restaurants. But restaurants were destination spots. You went to eat and then you went home. A whole other concept might be to create a destination neighborhood, where you could take care of all of your errands in one fell swoop.

I made a list of the businesses I frequented: coffee shop, dry cleaner, veterinarian, paint store, bookstore, drug store, shoe repair. I scratched out the last one because there was a very good chance it was too specific to me and my often-inherited estate sale wardrobes, but then changed my mind and wrote it again. Like so many other crafters, good cobblers were scarce. Besides, even new shoes needed TLC now and then.

Once I had a comprehensive list, I started on sketches. First was an exterior of a white building with a white slab roof. I glanced up at the rubble and spotted a pile of concrete tile with a diamond pattern in it. I sketched it onto the exterior street facing façade, and then on either side, added red beams that caged in the roof line. Above the roof, I drew a facsimile of the blue metal arrow and white oval sign that lay in the pile in front of me, and then lettered DRY CLEANER in the blank space. On the next page, I started with a circular building and sketched in stools around the perimeter.

I mocked up several sketches and then stood up and walked closer to the pile to see what I'd missed. It wasn't until I was about twenty-five yards from my belongings that I realized I wasn't alone.

# TEN

The man who'd entered the park while I talked to Lora stood at the end of the quarry. Three men stood behind him. I'd been so engrossed in my work I hadn't even noticed them, though their presence inside the quarry with me—not on the outer edges looking in—told me they'd been there awhile. As he approached me, he smiled, revealing a mouth filled with crooked teeth yellowed from smoking, a fact confirmed by the scent of nicotine that grew stronger as he closed the gap between us.

"Hello," he said. "Pretty lady in the quarry. What a lucky day for us." His words were over enunciated in a way that suggested English wasn't his first language, though there was no accent to confirm my suspicion.

He was a few feet in front of me. I stood rooted to the ground. "I was just leaving," I said.

"I don't think so," he said. "Pretty lady is all alone. That's unfortunate. I will fix for you. Pretty lady now has a date for the afternoon. Pretty lady has four dates for this afternoon."

Behind him, the other men chuckled. One of them said, "Save something for us, Benji."

He turned his head to the side. "Give us a little privacy, boys. You'll have your turn in a moment."

My fear alert went on high. Even though I'd told Hudson and Jimmy where I was going, I was alone. If I yelled, the only people who would hear me were the ones standing in my path. My personal belongings were on the rock where I'd been sitting and sketching, easily seventy-five feet from where I stood. My phone and anything I might have used as a weapon to defend myself quite literally out of my reach.

"Pretty lady is all alone. I could think of lots of ways to keep pretty lady company."

I felt like I'd been punched in the gut. It was my worst fear. Adrenaline coursed through me. I didn't know how much of what the man said was for scare tactics, but it was successful. There were four of them and one of me and I didn't like the odds. I also didn't like their inferences.

The skeletal man stepped close enough for me to pick up the scent of body odor. Involuntarily, my stomach clenched and I gagged. I put my hand to my face and stepped backward.

"What, don't you want a date?" he asked.

"I already have a date," I said.

"Funny, I don't see anybody here." He looked over my head. He reached his hand out and slipped his fingers under the zig zag hem of my top. Nausea and fear and rage swept over me.

I had a split second to act. I tightened my left arm and brought it up fast, knocking him under his chin. His head snapped back. Caught unprepared, he stumbled. I stepped forward and kneed him in the groin. He yelled and bent forward, too late. I turned around and ran away from him, across the quarry. He'd recover in a couple of seconds and be after me, and between him and his three friends and me and my occasionally bum knee, the odds were in his favor.

I scrambled through the mess of wreckage in the quarry, the shortest distance between two points being a direct line and not a wide circle around Jimmy's fixtures. Behind me, I heard cursing. I kept moving forward, but tripped twice. A length of metal scraped my leg, leaving a gash in my pale flesh. As I got closer to the rock where I'd set up camp to sketch, I got ready to grab what I could. My hand closed around the strap of my bag. The base of the bag fell against the sketch pad and knocked it to the ground. I had to sacrifice it.

I kept moving up the makeshift steps that had been carved out of the wall of the quarry, occasionally bending forward and using my hands in the dirt to help with traction and balance. I didn't hear anyone behind me, but I didn't stop. When I reached the top, a new burst of adrenaline propelled me to the Jeep. I scrambled inside, dumped my bag on the passenger seat, found the key, and then took off toward the river. I gripped the wheel tightly to stop my hands from shaking.

Hudson was alone under the pavilion when I arrived. He had a purple bandana rolled up and tied around his forehead, keeping his hair away from his face. "Hey, Lady," he said. "I was about to come looking for you."

I climbed out of the Jeep. His expression changed and he jogged to me. "What happened?"

"I had—there were—I'm okay," I stammered. I felt vulnerable, exposed. I looked back at Hudson. I didn't want to worry him. I didn't want to be any more trouble than I'd been. I turned around and looked at the parking lot, still afraid the men had followed me. We were alone.

Hudson looked down at my leg. "You're bleeding." He scooped me up and carried me to the picnic area, and then set me down on a table. "What happened?"

"I think I just met a couple of the locals," I said.

He looked the direction I'd come. "Where?"

"At the quarry." Being in the wide open space of the riverside with Hudson, the residual adrenaline converted to inappropriate giddiness. "You should see the other guys," I said.

"Guys? More than one?"

And then, the house of giddy collapsed. The almost suffocating fear that I'd felt in the quarry shivered over my bare skin and I wrapped my arms around myself. Hudson pulled me close and held me against his chest. "You're safe now," he said. "Do you know how you cut your leg?"

"I think I scraped against an old sign. I'm going to need a tetanus shot, aren't I?"

He uncapped a bottle of water and poured it onto my blood-caked leg. The water turned a faint shade of pink and ran down my calf. The scrape was about three inches long, but not as deep as I originally thought. "Yes," he said. "Better safe than sorry."

Talking to Hudson helped bring down my heart rate, but I couldn't shake the feeling I was still being watched. Had I not gotten out of there when I did, any number of bad things might have happened. The immediate tangible threat of danger had passed, but the sense I'd created a bigger one in its wake was left in its place.

If Hudson wanted more details about what had happened in the quarry, he respected my silence enough not to press for them. He checked the GPS on his phone and followed the directions, leading us to the local hospital. Minutes later I followed an orderly named Omar to a semi-private cubicle where I came into contact with one very large needle.

Two hours and one tetanus shot later, I was sent on my way. Hudson was waiting in the lobby. He put his hand out. "Everything okay?"

"Everything is okay," I said. "Should we get going?"

"Not so fast." He stretched his arm out toward me and I fell into step with his arm around me. "We haven't had much alone time alone since we got here."

"You're the one who wanted to stay with your sister," I joked.

"Not my best idea." He put his finger under my chin and raised my face. "Is there anything you want to talk about?"

"We can talk later. I don't like hospitals. Let's get out of here first." I knew he wanted to know the details of what had happened, but I'd finally succeeded in shaking the feeling that the men who'd threatened me were close by. I changed the subject. "Did you make any headway today?"

"Nope. Jimmy called it quits early. I think he's getting lost in the weeds of this project. We're going to get an early start tomorrow before it gets too hot." He grew quiet for a moment. "He wanted me to get you from the quarry before he left. I think he felt guilty. I told him you're a lot more independent than he thought and you'd call it quits when you were ready. I should have listened to him."

"I had a pretty productive day. I sketched out some ideas for him." For the first time since running from the quarry, I remembered the sketchpad that I'd left behind. "I left the sketches behind when I ran, but maybe I can describe them to him."

"He could use a visionary right about now. Whatever you designed, I'm sure he'll love it."

We walked out to the Jeep and I climbed in. Before shutting my door, Hudson pressed his finger into the flesh on my upper arm. "You got some sun."

I looked down at my skin. The bright sun made it hard to notice, but when I peered in the neckline of my top, I could see the developing tan line. "I wore sunscreen too. The sun's a little stronger out here than at home."

"No worries. Emma has two aloe plants at the house. Best thing for it." He walked around to the other side of the Jeep and climbed in next to me. "She came to the job site around lunch time. Dropped off some sandwiches. Did you eat?"

"Not unless you count the eraser on the end of my pencil."

"Then you must be hungry. I saved you a ham and cheese."

I ate half of the sandwich while Hudson drove back to Jimmy and Emma's house. I stared out the open window, taking in house after house, enjoying the clean lines and the unique desert landscaping. Soon we were bumping along the winding road where we'd had the accident.

Hudson slowed considerably, probably because he was thinking about it too. We passed the hairpin turn without incident, but as it turned out, that didn't mean we were in for an easy evening. Red and blue flashing lights announced the presence of the police at Emma and Jimmy's house before we pulled into the driveway.

Two Palm Springs Police vehicles sat behind Emma's mint-green convertible and an unfamiliar gray sedan. Hudson swung the Jeep around until it was parallel parked alongside the front hedge next to the mailbox. We both got out and approached the front door. Instinctively, I grasped Hudson's hand. He squeezed back.

Emma held the door open and Jimmy stood behind her with his hands on her shoulders. They both wore expressions of alarm. Whatever reason the police were here, it wasn't because something had happened to one of them. I relaxed, but only slightly.

Officer Buchanan stepped out from inside the door. "Mr. James, Ms. Night," he said. "We've been waiting for you."

"For us?" Hudson asked. "I was with Jimmy at the river."

"Not you. Ms. Night."

"But I saw you today." Everybody looked at me, and I realized I hadn't told any of them about my midday detour to the police station. I looked at Hudson. "I'll explain later," I said.

"No need to wait until later," said a man I hadn't met yet. "Ms. Night, I'm Detective Drayton." He wore a tan suit, light blue dress shirt, and navy blue necktie. Tortoise-shell Ray Ban sunglasses shielded his eyes, making it hard to gauge his expression. His hair was soft brown, lighter in the front as if he spent time in a swimming pool and the sun had bleached it out. He had a deep tan. He took off his sunglasses and scanned everybody's faces until his gaze rested on mine.

He held out his hand and I shook it. "After you left the station, we got a call from a couple who was hiking around some trails by the quarry. They wanted to report a body."

Jimmy's hands tightened on Emma's arms. Her face was pale, but she did not seem shocked by the news. The officers must have had a chance to fill them in before we arrived.

"The body was bloated and the lungs were full of water. It was pretty obvious it'd been submerged for an extended period of time."

"What does this have to do with Madison?" Hudson asked.

Drayton paused for one last second, in case we needed any more bombshells. "The body was tangled up with a couple of broken branches and a white straw hat with multicolored tassels. Looks like you were telling the truth about the body you saw in the river."

# ELEVEN

The room fell silent. I was pretty sure we were all thinking the same thing. Buchanan looked embarrassed. Drayton continued to speak. "The medical examiner is testing samples of the water in his lungs against the river to be sure, but based on your 911 call, we'd like to get more details from you about what you saw."

"Why didn't the officers find the body yesterday?" I asked.

"There were rope marks on the victim's ankles. It's too early to know, but the ME thinks he was tied to something to weigh him down. Add in the water current and you have a body with an unpredictable pattern of movement. Whoever did this didn't think things through very well. The body washed up about two hundred yards past Mr. McKenna's job site. I doubt that was the plan."

Next door, a dog barked repeatedly. "That sounds like Rocky," I said to Hudson.

Emma overheard me. "It is. I didn't want Heather to hear this so I asked her to take Rocky next door. Jo's watching them."

"I'd really like him to be here with me," I said.

Emma seemed to understand. "Of course. Jimmy, do you want to come with me? I think maybe Heather should see us together right now."

Jimmy's eyes cut to mine almost imperceptibly, and then to the police. "Sure, good idea," he said. The two of them went through the house and out the back door.

Hudson spoke up. "Detective, while I'm sure Madison likes knowing she didn't imagine the body in the water, it seems awfully strange for you to make a trip out here to tell her she was right."

"He didn't come out here to tell me I was right. Did you, Detective?" I asked.

"Ms. Night, you believed all along you saw a body. It's too soon for us to tell where the crime took place, so for now, we're treating the pier as the crime scene. It would make my job a little bit easier if you could tell me what you remember."

"Of course I'll cooperate," I said. "Would you like me to come to the station tomorrow?"

"I'd rather start right now," he said. "Is there a good place for us to talk?"

"We can sit in the living room," Hudson said.

The detective turned to Hudson. "I'd like to talk to Ms. Night alone," he said.

I put my hand on Hudson's forearm. "It's for the best."

Hudson looked back and forth at us. "I'll be out back."

Buchanan and Truman followed Hudson. Seconds later, I heard the sliding glass door open and shut. Drayton gestured toward the sofa. "Have a seat."

"First I'd like a glass of water. Can I get you anything?"

"No, thank you."

I went to the kitchen, poured a glass of water and dug two small doggie snacks out of the cabinet where I'd hid them. I returned to the living room and relaxed (as much as I could, considering the circumstances) on the sofa.

"Ms. Night, I probably don't have to tell you this whole thing is an embarrassment to our police force. You did the right thing by calling the police when you saw the body. Now we're in the unfortunate position of having to piece together the scene of discovery a day after the fact. I'd like to ask for your help in doing so."

"I already said I'd help," I said. That's when I noticed his cell phone, face up on the coffee table, glowed with the image of a microphone. "Am I being recorded?"

"We both are."

I nodded. Detective Drayton was putting on record the fact

that his department had screwed up. I wondered if that was standard procedure here in Palm Springs or if there was something more behind his action.

"Can you walk me through what you remember from yesterday before you saw the body?"

"Yes." I took a sip of water and then held the glass between my hands while I spoke. I recounted arriving late at the river, walking the length of the pier and waving to the men on the other side. "I was waving my hat to get their attention and I dropped it. It fell into the water and I was trying to figure out how to get it out when I saw it."

"The body?"

"Not quite. I didn't know it was a body at first. I saw movement under the surface. It wasn't anything noticeable, just enough for me to realize I saw something. I kept watching because I didn't know what had caught my attention. That's when I saw a pale face staring up at me. The eyes were blank and the hair moved back and forth under the surface."

"Then what?"

"Once I processed I was looking at a body, I tried to get Hudson and Jimmy's attention. There was no way for them to hear me so I backed away from the pier and called 911."

"About how much time passed between your phone call and Officers Buchanan and Truman arriving?"

"I don't know—I wasn't timing it. The usual amount of time, I think." As soon as it was out of my mouth, I froze up and stared at the recording cell phone. "I don't mean to imply I call 911 a lot. I call it when there's an emergency. I've been involved in some unfortunate situations in the past." I flashed back to a situation two years ago when the police suspected Hudson of committing a ten-year-old murder. We hadn't known each other as well as we did now, but even then, I'd been sure of his innocence. I hadn't cooperated that time and it had almost cost me my life.

"Ms. Night, you can relax. Your reputation is not being questioned. Officer Buchanan gave me the name of the police captain in Dallas and I spoke to him too. He suggested this conversation. I'm not here because you did anything wrong. I'm here because we did."

"How is he?" I asked. "Lieutenant Allen—I mean, Captain Allen."

"He seems like a nice guy. Having a hard time adjusting to being behind a desk and not out in the field, but he's got twenty-five years of service under his belt and sounds to me like he was due for either a promotion or retirement. Hard to tell which way people are going to go when they hit the quarter of a century mark. Must be police work is in his blood."

"Must be," I said. I sensed we were no longer alone and I looked up.

Hudson stood in the doorway. "I thought you'd like to know Rock is out back with us. Do you want him in here? Or are you just about finished up?"

Drayton said, "Is Rock your dog?"

"Yes."

He looked at his watch. "Are you okay if we power through for another fifteen minutes or so?"

"If I say no, does it undo everything I said about cooperating with the police?"

"Fifteen minutes," he repeated.

I looked at Hudson. "Fifteen minutes."

"Okay."


Fifteen minutes turned out to be enough to cover the duffel bag and empty coffee cup but not much more. Drayton's expression changed from one of curiosity to slight confusion. His brows pulled together, creating two small dimples above the inside of each. His eyes narrowed and he changed position, from sitting straight up to leaning forward.

He picked up his phone and spoke directly into it. "Talk to Buchanan about duffel and coffee cup," he said, and then turned the phone off. "That should do it for tonight. I have a team at the river to collect any evidence they might find, though I'm not confident we'll find anything. Sun's pretty severe these days, and at night, lots of critters come around the river to take whatever is left behind."

"Detective, you said the hikers found the body at the quarry, right? Something happened today that might be related." I lowered myself to the sofa again and put my hand on the bandage on my calf. "I was at there, at the quarry. Jimmy's been using the dump site to store the fixtures he purchased in Salton and I wanted to see what he had. A couple of men approached me while I was there."

"Men?" he said, his eyes cutting to the bandage. "You were attacked?"

"I was threatened, but I'm the one who did the attacking."

"I don't follow."

I'd been over the attack in my mind too many times by now and I knew that those men had something very bad in mind when they found me. A niggling voice in my head made me question if my reaction had been in line with the situation, or if, like my dreams, it had been a side effect of the events I hadn't yet dealt with from Texas.

"There were four men in the quarry. They approached me. The main guy, the leader, he said things. Unpleasant things. I don't think I imagined the threat."

"Describe this guy."

"I first saw him yesterday at the Parks and Rec office. I got the feeling he knew the woman who worked there—Lora? He was tall and gaunt, thinning black hair slicked back over his head. He had a pronounced forehead and cheekbones. He looked like a skeleton with skin on it, no flesh, no softness. His teeth were yellow, probably from smoking. And he smelled pretty bad. One of the guys called him Benji."

"Benji Nalder," Drayton said. He stood a little straighter, and I sensed the name meant something to him. He looked at his phone, which hadn't caught the last part of our conversation.

He stepped away from the table. I followed him to the door. "Detective, your officers probably told you I came to the precinct today. I found a set of keys jammed between the slats of the pier, right by where the duffel bag was. The keys had a Chevy emblem on the fob, and I think maybe the truck belongs to the victim."

"Where are the keys now?" he asked.

"Officer Buchanan advised me to take them to the Parks and Rec Lost and Found."

He slid the back door open and flagged Buchanan over to us. "I need you to go to Parks and Rec and follow up on a set of keys."

Buchanan looked at me. "Are these the keys you told me about this afternoon?"

"Yes."

Buchanan looked at Drayton. "Parks and Rec closed at five. I'll go see her first thing in the morning."

Detective Drayton nodded and turned back to me. "Thank you for your time." He looked at the backyard. "Tell Mr. and Mrs. McKenna I'm sorry to have interrupted their evening."

A few seconds later, he and the other two officers passed through the interior and out the front door toward the gray sedan. As Detective Drayton's trousers brushed against the door of the car, a film of dirt transferred onto his clothes and revealed a shiny streak of metal on the side of the car. Drayton stopped outside of the car and smacked his hand against the side of his clothes a couple of times, and the dirt fell away like stale pixie dust past its expiration date.

Seconds later, Rocky bounded around the corner of the house. I scooped him up and snuggled my face into his fur. Emma appeared behind him shortly. "I heard the front door open and thought you might be finished. Rocky and I have been waiting for him to drive away." She reached her hand up and ruffled his fur. He wriggled around in my arms a bit, and then jumped back down and hopped around my feet.

"Thanks. I honestly don't know what I'd do without Rocky," I said. "I don't have family like you do. This little guy is my cornerstone." I watched him run circles around my ankles. Mortiboy jumped up onto the inside window sill and Rocky ran over and yipped. "If we don't want him to sound the alarm through the neighborhood, we better get outside with Jimmy and Hudson."

"Madison, wait." Emma stood still, as if rooted to the yard like a palm tree. She stared intently at Rocky. "Can I talk to you? I feel like I'm going to burst and I need to confide in someone."

"Is this about this morning?" I asked. "Emma, I'm the last person to judge you. Relationships are hard. I just about gave up on them before your brother convinced me it was worth taking a chance. Maybe Jimmy needs some help with his anger, but if you want, we can stay elsewhere while we're here so you don't have the added stress of guests on top of everything else."

She looked up at me, her eyes filled with tears. "It's not about this morning. Madison, I'm the one to blame for everything that's gone wrong since you got here."

The unshed tears gave way and ran down her face. She seemed less in control of her emotions than last night, but I couldn't let her punish herself. I pulled her in for a hug and patted her back. "Emma, you can't torture yourself. There are two of you in this relationship. If something is wrong, there are two people to blame, not one."

"No, you don't understand." She pulled away from me and swiped at her eyes with her fist. "My marriage is over. I've been having an affair, and I'm pretty sure he's the body you found in the river."

# TWELVE

Emma's confession was unexpected. I knew she was upset about the fight with Jimmy and now the police being at her house. Her guilt seemed to cause the two incidents to blur.

She put her hand on my arm. "I shouldn't have said anything, but I can't keep it in anymore. Don't tell anybody. Not even my brother."

"I don't want to keep secrets from Hudson."

"Please?"

"Fine. The affair is your personal business, and other than that, I'm not sure there's anything to tell. What makes you think you know the victim?"

"While you were inside, the officers were talking about a bag they found on the pier. When he and I used to meet, he always had a bag with him."

I noticed that she refrained from using her lover's name, but I didn't press for details. "What kind of bag?" I asked. People carried all sorts of bags with them and Emma overhearing that the victim was found with a bag was far from a positive ID. I'd seen the bag myself, on the pier the day I originally saw the body. I'd know from her details if it was the same one.

"It was olive drab, canvas. Like the kind you get at an army surplus store."

It sure sounded like the same bag.

"They said it was empty," she continued. "I—I've seen that bag before, but it was full of pills. He's a—he's a doctor, and one time, when he was here, I told him one of my prescriptions was low. He said he'd bring me a refill. He wanted the empty bottle and I gave it to him."

Emma was obviously upset, and having confessed her deepest, darkest secret to me was having a cathartic impact on her. Warning bells were going off in my head, indicators that the behavior of her doctor friend seemed far from ethical, but I didn't think it was the time for a lecture.

I didn't like being in a position where I knew more than I should, especially when it involved the police. "If you're sure it's him, then you need to tell the detective," I said.

She shook her head. "I can't. I mean, what am I supposed to say? They haven't identified the body yet, and nobody knows about us. Hudson told me you have experience with this kind of thing. How long do I have to pretend everything is normal?"

"The police are under no obligation to report in to us. Once they confirm the identity of the body, they'll notify his family." I hesitated for a moment. "Was he married too?"

"Not anymore."

"The job of the police is to investigate the crime. They're a little behind because of the amount of time that lapsed between the murder and discovery of the body, so they have to do what they can now."

"So how will I know what's going on?"

"You won't."

Her eyes, still damp with tears, bounced back and forth between my own. I sensed her desperation, but didn't know if it was rooted in fear of having her affair discovered or something worse. *She's Hudson's sister*, a voice in my head said. *She has a daughter and she's opened her home to you.*

"Have you tried calling him?"

Emma shook her head. "He told me not to call him. We always met at the antique marketplace by the Moroccan baskets. Otherwise, it was too risky."

"Then all you can do is wait." I took her hands in mine and squeezed them. "When the police identify the body, they'll notify his family. After they do, they'll release his identity to the media. You watch the local news. You read the paper and the internet. There will be updates as they happen. Once this becomes public knowledge, the community will demand information and the police will have to answer to them."

"I'm so scared," she said. She started to cry again and I hugged her. "If anybody finds out what I did, my life will be over."

After Emma, Jimmy, and Heather had turned in, Hudson and I stretched out in the hammock out back, him at one end and me at the other. Mortiboy sat on his chest and Rocky curled up by my side. Hudson's fingertips were just inside the hem of my dress, strumming gently on my thigh. To make room for the four of us, he left one leg on the ground and, with his toe, slowly moved the hammock back and forth. The only sound was that of the animals' even breathing and a couple of crickets chirping in the grass near the house.

Hudson hadn't asked for details about my conversation with the detective or the attack at the quarry, but I felt his unspoken questions in the air. "There were four men," I said quietly. "I don't know where they came from or how they knew I was there. The police said the body was found at the quarry, and I keep thinking maybe the men thought I saw something or knew something."

"Did they hurt you?"

"They scared me." I stared up at the dark midnight blue sky. It was like a swath of velvet draped over the top of the trees, speckled with stars that looked like glitter. "Maybe that's all they wanted to do. I didn't wait around to find out."

"Did you tell the police?"

"Yes." I lapsed into silence again. "You know what's weird?" I said. "I think I was happier when I started to believe I was wrong about what I saw." I stroked my hand over Rocky's fur. He shifted his tiny furry body and his back paw popped through one of the holes in the hammock. He opened his eyes, tipped his head, pulled his foot out, and rolled onto his back with his paws in the air. I moved my hand to his belly and kept petting.

"I hate to say it, but I think we all were. Not because anybody wanted you to be wrong, but..." Hudson's voice trailed off. He put his hands behind his head and stared up at the stars. The sun had dropped, but the hot desert temperature had barely changed. "I don't think I've seen Emma this shaken up since Jimmy put a frog in her sleeping bag at camp."

I laughed. "I didn't realize they went back that far."

"His family lived down the street from ours." He swatted at a fly buzzing around us. "We sure got into a lot of trouble together. There was always something between him and Emma. I didn't like it at first—my best friend starts to date my sister. Brought out all sorts of protective feelings. But Emma's got a mind of her own. If she wants to do something, she's going to charge ahead and do it no matter what the repercussions might be."

"Was this in Dallas?"

"Yeah. Mostly kid stuff, but the older we got, the higher the stakes. After our parents died, we moved in with my grandmother. There wasn't money for both of us to go to college. You already know what happened to me. Being under suspicion of murder changed a lot about my life."

Hudson was referring to his past. Being a good Samaritan had put him in the wrong place at the wrong time, and while no one had been able to prove he was guilty, suspicion of murder had hung over his head for two decades. During that time he'd learned who he could trust and who he couldn't and maintained a quiet existence in order to avoid town gossip about what people thought he'd done.

"When you told me about your grandmother raising you, you didn't mention Emma."

"Emma went away to college instead of me. I think my grandmother wanted to get her out of Dallas to protect her from the gossip."

"Did it work?"

"I don't know. She never came back. Don't tell Emma I said this, but Gram hoped Emma's world would open up and she'd see there was something bigger for her out there. But four years later, she and Jimmy reconnected and they've been together ever since."

We lapsed into silence. The swaying of the hammock became rhythmic, and I closed my eyes. Erratic sleep was taking its toll on me, and the high-low of emotions that came with the visit from the detective had left me on edge. I dozed off, and then jerked awake when fragmented images from the memories I'd tried to block filtered into my subconscious mind.

"What happened?" Hudson asked. He sat up on his side of the hammock and put his hands on my calves.

"Nothing," I said. "I must have fallen asleep."

"Let's get you inside. It's been a long day, and it wouldn't be the worst thing in the world to wind things down."

Hudson lifted Mortiboy and held him to his chest. I rolled to my side away from Rocky. As soon as I created vacant space, Rocky rolled into the center of the hammock. He scrambled to stand up and his paws popped through the loose weave of the rope again. He tried unsuccessfully to pull his paws back out and whimpered. I scooped him up and kissed his head. The four of us went into the house and locked the back door behind us.

Hudson showered first. I wandered around the guest bedroom, lining his and my sneakers up under the edge of the bed, moving our dirty clothes into an empty basket we were temporarily using as a hamper, and replacing Rocky's emergency pee pad with a fresh one. It seemed as though we'd all been stressed out since we arrived in Palm Springs.

I hadn't given much thought to Hudson's stresses since arriving. What I'd originally thought to be a comfortable family arrangement was fraught with trouble: his sister, her husband. Their marital challenges. A nine-year-old girl. Two pets who barely tolerated each other on their own turf, let alone the unfamiliar surroundings of Palm Springs.

And now, a murder.

From the first time I'd met him, Hudson had demonstrated a calm demeanor. He rolled with the punches and dealt with drama when it came around. We'd known each other for four years before I even knew about his past. I could think of only one occasion when he'd lost his cool to me, and I'd long forgiven him after learning the circumstances. It might have been the night he introduced me to his own demons that I first realized I was falling in love with him. At the time, I was far from ready for a relationship—I'd pretty much decided it would be me and Rocky for the rest of our lives. My idol, Doris Day, had had her own romantic challenges and had found that happiness came as easily when you surround yourself with animals as when you surround yourself with men. Maybe she hadn't said it quite like that, but still.

So Hudson knew about my past and I knew about his, but there was still a whole lot of gray area neither of us spoke about. Even though I was forty-eight to his forty, it felt like he'd lived far more than I had. Both of our parents had passed away. I was an only child turned only woman. I grew up in Pennsylvania, but moved to Dallas when I was forty-five. He grew up in Dallas and told me his grandmother had raised him. He'd never mentioned Emma when he talked about those days. He once asked me why I believed he was innocent when even his friends had thought him to be guilty. Had Emma—and Jimmy, now that I thought about it—been in the camp that distanced themselves from him at a time when he'd most needed their support?

I didn't want to tell Hudson, but I was nervous about trying to fall asleep. If anything was going to trigger the nightmares, the reality of having seen a body floating in the river would probably top the list. We switched places, him freshly shampooed and washed, smelling of soap and laundry detergent, and me in need of shower therapy and a bar of Happy soap like Doris Day's character advertised in *The Thrill of it All*.

Freshly scrubbed and dressed in a white eyelet PJ top and matching bloomers, I made a decision. The pills were in case of emergency, and while I'd made a promise to myself I wouldn't become dependent on them, I knew waking the house up with my screaming, today of all days, wasn't an option.

I patted my hands over my belongings. The pills weren't there. I double checked my makeup case, and then stepped out of the bathroom and rooted through my luggage.

"What's wrong?" Hudson asked.

"I was going to take a sleeping pill, but I can't find my prescription."

"It's in the medicine cabinet. I found it on the floor. Probably fell out of your bag."

I went back into the bathroom and slid the medicine cabinet open. My prescription sat on the second shelf between a bottle of aspirin and an unopened package of Q-Tips. I took the prescription bottle out of the cabinet and the back of the shelf fell forward, revealing a secret compartment. I shifted the rest of the items out of the way and revealed a cabinet filled row upon row with amber pill vials similar to mine except with prescriptions in Emma's name.

Curiosity took hold of me. I took a bottle from the shelf and checked the label. The prescriptions were for Valium. There were easily thirty bottles. They were all full. I'd never seen so much Valium in one place in my life.

The prescribing physician was Dr. Albert Hall, the same doctor Officer Buchanan had suggested I talk to in order to deal with my stress. Emma had said her affair had been with a doctor who offered to fill her prescriptions, and it seemed like they were one and the same. If Emma was correct about the identity of the victim, the doctor's days of counseling were over.

# THIRTEEN

The sleeping pill dropped me into a deep slumber and left me groggy and lethargic the next morning. I had a vague memory of Hudson waking me, only for me to roll over and fall back asleep. Palm Springs was turning out to be more than a vacation from my life in Dallas, it was a break from my entire routine. Creature of habit that I was, I wasn't sure I liked it.

I pulled my blonde hair back into a high ponytail and changed into a turquoise and white sleeveless dress with a wide pleat down the front (McCalls 8755). I tied a turquoise ribbon around my head to hold my hair back, and then led Rocky down the hallway and let him out the front door. He raced a few feet and then did his business next to a small row of succulents. He'd had a chance to run around the backyard the previous day, but like me, he was sorely off his exercise regimen. Already the temperature felt like the inside of an oven.

"Tomorrow," I promised him. "I'll get up early and we'll go for a walk." He sniffed a row of plants and then ran back into the house.

Jimmy sat at the dining room table typing on a laptop. "Help yourself to coffee," he said. "Hudson went out for bagels."

"Where's Emma?"

"She took Heather to school."

I filled a mug with coffee and removed an English muffin from the package on the counter. "What's the plan for today?" I asked. "Back to the river?"

Jimmy looked up from his computer. "The river is off limits."

There was a hard edge to his tone. "The police went this morning to look for evidence connected to your body. The whole project is on hold indefinitely." He looked back at his computer screen.

I fought to keep my tone light. "It's not 'my body.'"

He looked up at me. "Yeah? Well, whoever's body it is, it's costing me money I don't have. If you hadn't seen it, probably nobody would have known it was there and we'd be making time on the job right now."

Jimmy's insensitive tone set me off. "Is that what you're worried about? Your timetable? A man was *killed*," I said, stressing the last word. "I had a moral obligation to report it to the police and they have a professional obligation to investigate the crime. I *know* you're not suggesting things would have been better if I had kept my mouth shut."

He slammed the laptop shut. "I know your type. I've known your type my whole life. You're just out for attention. You think we'll all find it cute you like Doris Day so much you dress like her. Ever since you got here it's been one thing after another. You got my wife looking at you and Hudson and thinking our life should be more like yours or like something out of a movie. You think you're the first woman to come along and catch Hudson's eye? Think again. I've known him since we were kids. There's been a long line before you. You better not play the victim card for too long or he's going to get bored."

"Is that what you think? I played a victim so Hudson would pay attention to me?"

"If you didn't want attention, you wouldn't be standing here in a stupid outfit some woman wore fifty years ago."

It took everything in me to remember I was in Jimmy's house, a supposed guest of his and Emma's hospitality. But I had control over my circumstances. Jimmy's words bit into me in a way I wasn't prepared to deal with. I set the mug down on the counter. "Thank you for making it clear how you feel." I walked down the hallway and threw everything I'd unpacked back into my suitcase. Seventeen minutes later, Rocky and I left.

Righteous indignation didn't carry me far. I knew approximately seven people in Palm Springs. Ruling out Jimmy, Emma, and anybody related to law enforcement, I ended up knocking on the door of the next-door neighbor.

Jo answered. Today she wore a white T-shirt and khaki Bermuda shorts. Her close-cropped hair was slicked down to her head in a way that suggested she'd recently showered. Her feet were bare.

"Madison, right?" she said.

"Yes. I'm sorry to bother you, but I have a—well, a pretty embarrassing favor to ask. Do you think you could give me a ride into town?"

She glanced at the giant turquoise suitcase next to my feet. "Trouble in paradise?" she asked. "Maybe it's contagious."

"Paradise is fine," I said, "but I think there's been a little too much togetherness. Hudson and I might be in town longer than we initially thought. I think the decent thing is to get a hotel room."

"If only all visitors were as considerate as you. Let me put on shoes."

I didn't know if Jimmy watched me walk to Jo's front door or not, and truthfully, I didn't care. I knew he was angry about the change to his timetable and the loss of money, but there were other ways to express his frustration. He'd been nothing but rude to me since I arrived, and I'd been independent for too long to sit back and take it.

Victim, my ass.

Jo slipped on a pair of flip flops and grabbed her keys. "Let's go." I followed her to the hatchback parked in her driveway. She unlocked the doors and moved a stack of colorful flyers from the passenger side seat to the back. Rocky and I climbed in and I held him on my lap. "You have a place in mind?" she asked.

"Not really. If you can drop me off at a Starbucks, I'll boot up my computer and find a motel that takes animals. Honestly, I know this is a bit much to ask of you."

"Honey, forget about it." She backed out of the driveway and took off down the narrow road. Soon we were on East Palm Canyon Drive. "You think I don't know what Jimmy is like? When I bought the house, I thought we'd become friends. Our girls were the same age and went to the same school. It would have made sense. But there was something off whenever we were together. It was like Jimmy didn't want Emma and me to spend any time together. Maybe single women intimidate him. I tried to bring it up to her, you know, girl talk, but she acted like it was all in my head. I finally got bored with the whole thing."

"I don't mean to pry, but you mentioned your divorce the other day. Is Gina's dad in the picture?"

"Not anymore, thank God." She rolled her eyes. "I bought the house with money from the settlement. He got off cheap. After the divorce was final I found out he'd slept with his receptionist and at least two different patients."

Something Jo had said earlier tickled at the back of my mind, and a series of facts slipped together into an unavoidable conclusion.

"You said he was a doctor, didn't you?"

"Psychiatrist. People say surgeons have a God complex, but psychiatrists are the absolute worst. He used to brag about how he knew everybody's secrets." She turned into the parking lot of a Tiki-themed motel. "This looks to be right up your alley. It has a pool too. A couple of friends of mine stayed here last year and gave it a thumbs up. Good price, especially in the off season."

"Thanks," I said. I opened the door. Rocky climbed out, but stayed close to the car. "Jo, when's the last time you talked to your ex?"

"Gosh, I don't know. I cut ties before the ink was dry on the divorce papers. He probably expected me to move out of Palm Springs, but the joke was on him."

"What joke?"

"You're looking at the new vocalist for the summer concert series at the music hall." She beamed. "I made sure they delivered a whole stack of programs to Albert's office too. Wish I'd been there to see the look on his face. One of these days, karma is going to catch up to him."

I didn't say what was running through my head. It seemed to me that something had already caught up with Dr. Albert Hall, and it was far more human than karma.

# FOURTEEN

As sure as I was that Jo's ex-husband was the murder victim, I couldn't be the one to tell her. The police, once they'd determined the victim's identity, would be knocking on her door. He was the father of her child, but, depending on the nature of their divorce, she'd probably be questioned as a suspect.

How long would it be before the police reached the same conclusion I had? I'd been privy to snippets of information I'd picked up since arriving in Palm Springs: the detective's recommendation I talk to the psychiatrist he talked to, Emma's suspicion that the doctor she was having an affair with was the man who'd been killed, and the row of prescription bottles in Emma's house. Jo and Emma seemed to have a friendly relationship, too. It was unclear if Jo knew—or cared—that her ex had been dallying with her neighbor. But because of everything I knew, links between confidences were growing and conclusions were being reached. I didn't like being at the epicenter of everybody else's secrets.

I had a choice. Call the police and offer up my theory, or let them investigate the crime themselves. Would it do anybody any good for me to claim to know the victim's identity? Not when the admission would require me to violate at least one person's trust. The medical examiner would reach the same conclusion, probably sooner rather than later. Add in what the police would piece together after a day at the river, including the abandoned SUV in the parking lot, and my information would be old news. It would impede the investigation, not help it along.

And frankly, considering I was standing outside of a motel and hadn't yet called Hudson to tell him what had happened or where I'd gone, it seemed more prudent to focus on the problem at hand.

Thanks to the fact that only people who have agreed to a vacation where they're also working for their friends/family appeared to come to Palm Springs in September, the motel was mostly vacant. When the manager heard about the animals, he gave me a suite with two queen-sized beds at the single bed rate. Somehow I knew both Rocky and Mortiboy would end up in whichever bed Hudson and I chose. I checked in, set up a corner for Rocky, and pulled out my phone. I'd missed two calls from Hudson.

"Hi," I said when he answered my return call.

"Madison, what's going on? I left to get bagels and when I came back the house was empty. All of your stuff was gone. Is there something I should know?"

So Jimmy had left the house too. That meant Hudson didn't know about the argument. Jimmy's accusation of my attention-seeking was still ringing in my ears, so I did the only thing I could to quiet them down. I took the high road. "This is our first getaway, right?"

"Right."

"I thought it should feel more like our first getaway. I packed up and checked us into a motel. I'm at Tiki Tropics on East Palm Canyon Drive."

"You're already there?"

"I wanted to surprise you."

"Color me surprised. Where are Rock and Mortiboy?"

"The motel allows pets. Rocky's with me, but I thought you'd like to be the one to bring Mortiboy."

"What about Emma and Jimmy?"

"I think Emma and Jimmy will be just fine on their own."

His voice dropped lower. "What about us?"

"I'm hoping we'll be just fine on our own too."

A beat of silence passed between us, an undercurrent I hadn't felt since we left Dallas. "The police told Jimmy the river is off limits temporarily while they scout the scene for evidence, so he asked if I'd be willing to head with him out to Salton Springs to pick up some more fixtures and signs. Right about now I wish I'd said no."

"We'll have plenty of time together tonight. The main reason we came here was to help Jimmy. You go with him. There's a local flea market I want to check out. If we divide and conquer, we'll both feel better about relaxing tonight."

"I didn't say anything about relaxing," Hudson said.

I smiled to myself. "Go do what you have to do. I'll tell the front desk you and Mortiboy are joining me so you can check in if you get here while I'm out."

"You think of everything, don't you?" he asked.

"I'm a little rusty on this relationship stuff, but I'm doing my best."

"I wouldn't want it any other way."

After we hung up, I cranked the air conditioning and unpacked. The room was a kitschy shrine to Polynesian Tiki culture from the fifties. The bed was trimmed with bamboo, and the headboard was covered in colorful bar cloth that mimicked the island feel. Framed paintings of Tikis hung along one wall. They were numbered and signed by a local artist. While the décor was charming, the size of the room was small. It had been one thing to agree to stay in a house owned by Hudson's sister. It was an entirely other thing to restrict ourselves to a motel room with little more than a couple of beds. I unpacked my overnight kit on the sink and left my sleeping pills next to the motel water glass.

Rocky appeared to have been affected by the overbearing heat. He lay on the center of one of the queen-sized beds with his chin resting between his paws and his hind legs spread out behind him. His turned-up little black nose whistled quietly as he breathed. I shifted my now-empty suitcase from the luggage stand to the hall closet, and Rocky watched me with mild interest. It was only a matter of time before I abandoned the pretense of moving into the room and joined him on the bed. I pulled my hair up off my neck and reclined, staring up at the ceiling.

"This is turning out to be quite a getaway, isn't it?" I asked him. I put my right hand on top of his back and he rolled against me. "I knew things were going to be complicated, but I never thought they'd get this complicated this fast." I closed my eyes and thought about everything that had happened since we'd arrived. The flipped Jeep, the body in the water, the arguments among Emma, Jimmy, and me, and the confrontation at the quarry. And then there were the bits and pieces of information I'd picked up randomly. Sitting here and waiting for everybody around me to get caught up with information and discover what I already knew was enough to make me want to scream.

There was another thought bothering me. My decision to get a motel room meant closer quarters for Hudson and me than at Emma's house. There would be no kitchen to escape to if I wanted to get up and avoid the nightmares. I wasn't going to want to take a sedative in order to sleep. But would the nightmares come back? Would I suffer through a replay of what had happened in Dallas yet again? Was everybody right in telling me I wouldn't start to get past the memories until I faced them head on, acknowledged what I'd lived through, and dealt with the emotional carnage surrounding the outcome?

I dug a business card that I'd been carrying around for several months out of my handbag. It had been given to me by Captain Washington before he'd retired. He'd been the first to suggest I seek counseling and had made arrangements for me to talk to the same psychiatrist the precinct used. Even though I wasn't at home, I felt like if I didn't set up an appointment now, I might never take the step. I was alone in a motel room. Nobody would know if I made the call.

I made the call.

A woman answered. "Good morning, Dr. Randall's office."

"Good morning. I'm Madison Night. I was given Dr. Randall's name for possible"—I paused, seeking the right word—"sessions."

"I'm sorry, Dr. Randall isn't accepting new patients at the moment. I can refer you to another doctor if you'd like."

"I was referred by the police captain," I said quickly. "He probably expected me to set something up before now, but he made the arrangements after what happened with the Lakewood Abductor."

"Can I place you on hold for just a moment?"

"Sure."

I put the phone on speaker and wandered the room. Soft jazz filtered through the phone. I opened the floor-to-ceiling curtains, exposing the view of the motel's pool two floors below. Lush green tropical plants were scattered about the pool deck next to Tiki-inspired planters and carved wooden statues. A few people reclined on bright orange poolside folding loungers, and a cluster of children jumped around the shallow end of the pool. I unlocked the balcony door and slid it open, immediately hit with a wall of heat. Rocky hopped past my feet to the balcony and stuck his nose between the white iron bars, and then turned around and went back inside. Perhaps when the sun went down, it would be nice to sit out here. Not now. I went back into the room and slid the door shut.

The jazz music was replaced with a male voice. "Ms. Night?"

"Yes, this is Madison Night."

"This is Dr. Randall. I understand you'd like to start working with me on your issues?"

*Work.* That's what therapists called the process of exploring the deep dark corners of our minds. "Yes," I said. "I don't know if you know who I am. Police Captain Washington suggested I talk to you. He arranged it after the abductions. I understand he made it mandatory for everybody on the force to talk to you about what happened, and because of my involvement he said he arranged for me to have the same privilege."

"Captain Washington retired last week. I don't foresee a problem, but I'll have to clear it through his replacement."

My breath caught in my chest. I should have seen this coming. After months of not talking, after the countless times I'd picked up the phone but hung up without dialing, after pretending nothing had changed while everything had changed, it seemed my mental wellbeing lay squarely in the hands of the former Lieutenant Tex Allen.

# FIFTEEN

*Tex*

Tex sat on the sofa, waiting for the doctor's return. He'd been reluctant about starting therapy, wondering if the other guys on the force would talk. But when Captain Washington retired, he'd made it mandatory that every member of the precinct get a psychological profile and follow up with a minimum of two sessions with Dr. Randall. Now, nobody could talk behind anybody's back because they were all in the same boat.

The public outcry after the string of abductions and murders around town had demanded the police force make changes. Like many of the other officers, Tex assumed Captain Washington's job was about to get a lot harder. The force had a unified mission to reestablish trust in the community, and that trust leveled a lot of attitude and testosterone. When Captain announced his retirement, it hadn't come as a surprise to anybody.

When Tex was named his replacement, it had.

Any time scandal hit a public office there were repercussions, and this was no different. The fact that Tex had been at the center of the scandal had been hard. Regardless of the emotions he'd cycled through, his vow to protect and serve the residents of Lakewood, Texas was stronger than ever. He had a front-row seat to how deep the community's trust in the police had been and how damaged it was now. When he stepped forward as a candidate for the position of Captain, it was with the full knowledge his job would become more about the image of the police force than being in the field. It had been a hard adjustment, but things change, life goes on. His own life had forked and he'd been on the brink of the dark side: alcohol, women, violence. As much as he hated to admit it, the sessions with Peter were helping.

They had an agreement. Peter would treat Tex's drop-in visits like those of a friend. They'd talk over coffee or lunch, occasionally over a beer at the local pub. The doc kept track of their time and billed the department accordingly, but Tex found it way easier to relax his guard when he acted like he was hanging out with a buddy. Occasionally, like now, Peter was called upon as Dr. Randall to handle emergency phone sessions with a patient, and that interrupted Tex's time. He didn't have a problem with it, because it maintained the illusion that allowed him to keep coming back.

Peter came back into the office. "Sorry about the interruption. New patient."

"I thought you weren't taking new patients?" Tex asked.

"Now that I'm busy treating the entire staff of the Lakewood Police Department, I don't have time for new patients."

Peter pumped a squirt of hand sanitizer into his palm and rubbed his hands together. For a psychiatrist, he had plenty of quirks, not the least of which included being a neat freak. Tex had gotten used to Peter's almost unconscious habits of wiping condensation from the bar, dusting off his chair with his handkerchief before sitting down, and tending to his numerous plants at exactly eleven fifteen. A couple of the other guys on the force referred to Peter as Felix Unger, but Tex kept that to himself. His shrink didn't have to know everything.

"Remind me when we're done I have some official police business to ask you about," Peter said.

"Fire away. I'm all out of issues for today."

"You might change your mind when you hear my question."

Tex leaned back and put his hands behind his head. "What's up? Is somebody giving you a hard time about their psych eval?"

"Not exactly." Peter picked up a stack of papers from the corner of his desk and tapped them a few times, lining up the edges. "That new patient I mentioned—she's a referral. From Captain

Washington." Peter slid the stack of papers into a clean file folder and set it on the shelf behind his desk. "One of your female friends."

"She?" Tex could think of only one female officer who his old captain would go to task for. His former sometimes girlfriend Donna Nast. She'd left the force a year earlier and started her own security company. "Nasty? Just don't schedule her anywhere near me. This town is entirely too small for the both of us."

Peter shook his head slowly and smiled. "Wrong one."

"Huh?"

"I wouldn't bring it up, except your position as Captain puts you in the unique position of approving or denying her request to start counseling."

"Who are you talking about?"

Peter's grin was a little too much like the Cheshire Cat. "Madison Night," he said. He waited a second. "You still think you're all out of issues today?"

# SIXTEEN

I had two choices: find another psychiatrist, or bite the bullet and call Tex. There was probably a third option in there somewhere, but I was an adult, and as such, I could tackle this head-on. The doctor said his office would follow up with me after confirming my request, but I couldn't just sit still and let this all transpire without reaching out to Tex myself. It was a phone call I should have made months ago, but seeing as I was alone for the next several hours, there appeared to be no time like the present.

I called Tex's cell. He didn't answer, which made things both easier and more strained. I'd been so worried about what to say to him that I hadn't rehearsed what I might say in the message. I disconnected the call and immediately regretted my action.

There was a good chance my psychological issues extended beyond PTSD.

I redialed the number. Four rings, and then the beep. "Hi," I said. "This is Madison. It's been a long time. I hear congratulations are in order. Good for you." I glanced at Rocky, who was back asleep. "I've been having some issues since, well, you know, and Captain Washington said he'd set things up so I could talk to the department psychologist. I understand the doctor has to get your approval now, so I'm hoping you're not mad about the fact I haven't called in five months. And if you are, please accept my apology. And if you're not," I paused again, "you should be, because if the tables were turned, I'd probably be mad at you. Because we're supposed to be friends or something, right?" I paused, feeling like the conversation had gotten away from me. "Okay, well, I have to run. Congratulations, Captain."

I hung up and stared at the phone. I would have been better not calling back.

I unpacked my clothes and then went to the bathroom. Rocky sniffed the corners of the room. My phone rang as I finished washing my hands. I answered it on the third ring. "Hello?" I answered.

"Madison Night. I was wondering if I'd ever hear from you again."

"Lieutenant Allen," I said.

"It's Captain Allen now."

"I heard. Doesn't have quite the same ring though."

When I'd first met Tex, he'd been investigating a body that had been under the wheels of my vintage blue Alfa Romeo. His casual, flirtatious manner had put me and my emotional boundaries on high alert. Since then, I'd made a conscious effort to refer to him by his title and not his nickname because it kept him at a distance. On more than one occasion, I'd taken great pleasure in telling off Lieutenant Tex Allen, and I suspected he hadn't minded a bit.

Truth was, Tex was as much to thank for my newfound willingness to be in a relationship as Hudson was. He knew how to push my buttons and offended me with his womanizing ways. He also treated me like an intellectual equal and sought out my advice and opinion. He'd stolen my car, put me under surveillance, and made me frequent a strip club. We were alike in ways I never would have imagined, but when Tex was at his lowest, he shut me out. Perhaps it was yet another way we were alike. It was never comfortable when someone held a mirror up to you and you could see your own flaws reflected in it.

"You can call me Lieutenant if you want. I kinda miss it."

"Those days are over. You gave that up when you accepted your promotion."

"I gave up a lot of things recently," he said. "I haven't been to Jumbo's Strip Club in months."

"Someone should give you a medal."

He laughed. "Man, I missed talking to you. So, what's up, Night? Staying out of trouble?"

"Not exactly." I sat down on the bed. "Can I get your opinion on something police-related?"

"Shoot." I stared out the open curtains trying to figure out where to begin. "Night? Are you still with me?" he asked.

"I'm in Palm Springs. With Hudson James. We came out here to do a job for his brother-in-law and—"

"And you saw a body in the river and now you're in the middle of a mess."

"Yep."

"When the police in Palm Springs answered your first call and didn't find a body, they weren't sure if they were dealing with a crackpot. They ran a background check. You have an unusual history when it comes to the police, so they called here to check up on you."

"Officer Buchanan said he talked to you."

"That was two days ago. I'm surprised I didn't hear from you then."

"You got a call about me from a strange police department. I'm surprised *you* didn't call *me*."

"Touché."

"Have you heard from Buchanan since that first call?"

"No, but I heard from Detective Drayton. What's going on out there, Night?"

I told Tex everything—well, almost. I told him about the Jeep tipping over and the empty duffel bag at the pier. I told him about the abandoned SUV, the parking tickets, and the body that had turned up days after I'd first seen the floater in the river. I told him about the keys wedged between slats of the pier, Emma's confession she was having an affair with her doctor, the prescription bottles hidden in her medicine cabinet, and the coincidence of the ex-wife living next door. I even told him about Jimmy's accusations that I was an attention seeker who had cost him work. I kept the confrontation at the quarry to myself so as not to confuse the details of the murder.

"What does James have to say about his sister's affair or the brother-in-law's accusations?"

"He doesn't know about either." I walked to the window and pushed the curtains aside. Bright sunlight spilled into the window, hot against my bare skin. Kids in the pool below batted a multicolored inflatable ball back and forth. Their laughter carried up to me.

"Why not?"

"Because I haven't told him. Okay?"

"No, it's not okay. Why haven't you told him?"

"I don't have to tell him everything."

"Night, take some advice from me. Open up and let the guy be a part of your life or you're going to end up alone."

It was an emotional sucker punch. "I have to go," I said.

"Call me back. We're not done talking about this."

I hung up. The phone rang almost immediately and I left the call unanswered. I took a few deep breaths, and then went to the bathroom and splashed cool water on my face. "Come on, Rocky, let's get out of here," I said. I clipped a turquoise leash onto his collar and locked the door behind me.


Palm Springs had what was known as the Buzz, a bunch of well-maintained trolleys that provided free access around the downtown area. They were white with brightly colored graphics that provided a whimsical nod to the mid-century vibe. Between sitting around a small motel room and braving the ninety-plus temperature, I chose the latter. The motel concierge pointed me in the direction of the nearest pick-up stop, and Rocky and I headed that direction.

In a matter of minutes, I regretted my decision. Ninety degrees, even in the desert, sapped me of my energy. I questioned how much work Jimmy and Hudson would get done at the nearby Salton Springs. If I didn't feel an obligation to participate in the project like Hudson had asked, I would have changed into my bathing suit and spent the day lounging by the pool. But I was tough when it came to scouting out flea markets and second-hand resources, and today would be a good day for bargains. Vendors would know only serious buyers would venture out in this temperature, and it was in everybody's best interest to strike an agreeable deal. And as luck would have it, the Buzz route to the flea markets had a stop two blocks from Dr. Hall's office.

I left the Buzz and carried Rocky until we reached the corner. He whimpered when I set him down on the hot sidewalk. We moved to the far right and stayed under the shade of the buildings until we reached a large pale yellow building with aqua doors. The roof was flat except for a copper incline that held solar panels aimed at the sun. I walked up the concrete path and short flight of stairs and entered the double doors with Rocky by my side. If there were signs that said "no pets allowed," I chose not to see them.

On the left-hand wall was a directory. Unlike my own doctor's office, this one displayed headshots of the physicians who occupied the building. I located Dr. Hall and studied the picture. The similarities between the pale, lifeless face I'd seen in the water and the attractive man who stared out at me were hard to spot, but I couldn't deny it was the same person.

A door opened next to me and a woman in a tight red dress came out. "Can I help you?" she asked.

"I'm looking for Dr. Hall's office," I said.

Her eyes swept me quickly and, from her expression, she was not impressed with McCalls pattern #8755. "Dr. Hall is on vacation," she said.

The doctor's ex-wife had described him as a womanizer who'd engaged in more than one office romance, and I was being sized up as competition. And while the woman's attitude was far from pleasant, she also wasn't in mourning. The photo on the wall had confirmed his identity to me. I didn't need anything else.

"What did you want to see him about?"

Despite the fact that we were in an empty hallway outside of a psychiatrist's office, the question was too personal to answer, so I feigned misunderstanding. "Him? I thought Dr. Hall was a woman." I looked down at Rocky. "My dog's been having a hard time with the heat and I thought—"

"Your dog?"

I bent down and scooped up Rocky. "Don't tell me I got that wrong too. Isn't Dr. Hall a vet?" I stroked Rocky's fur. There's very little in this world less threatening than a middle-aged woman holding her dog like a baby.

The woman's expression softened. "There aren't any vets in this building," she said. "But I hope he feels better." She reached her hand out and ruffled his fur. I smiled again and carried him out.

Four minutes later we were back on the Buzz on the way to the flea market. The seats were all full, so we stood. I kept one hand on the guide rail and the other on Rocky's leash.

So Dr. Hall was on vacation. Nobody was looking for him. No wonder he hadn't been reported missing. Assuming the women in his life knew they shared him with others, none of them would be waiting at home with a hot casserole either. The most popular man in town was dead and I was the only one who knew.

Except for the murderer.

The Buzz rounded a corner and my phone rang. I held onto a vertical chrome pole for balance. Almost as soon as the phone stopped ringing, it started again. I looped Rocky's leash over my wrist and pushed it up to my elbow, and then pulled out my phone.

"Hello?"

"It's Emma. Have you heard from Hudson?"

"Not since this morning. He and Jimmy went to Salton Springs for the day. I got the feeling they're going to work as long as they can stand the heat."

"Forget about the heat. The guys got into a fight with some of the locals. I don't know how bad things got, but Jimmy and Hudson just checked themselves into the emergency room."

# SEVENTEEN

The trolley turned a corner and I was thrown off balance. I dropped my phone and grabbed the pole with both hands to steady myself. Rocky hopped out of the way and then looked up at me, scared. The trolley pulled over and a few people got off. I scooped up my phone and dropped into a newly vacated seat. Rocky's leash wound around my leg. I didn't know where I was headed, but I was no longer worried about getting to the flea market.

"Emma?" I said into the phone. I swiped the screen. The call had dropped. I called her back, but she didn't answer. I tried twice and then called Hudson. He didn't answer either. The trolley slowed to a stop and I got off.

Emma answered my third call.

"I'm sorry I hung up," she said. "Jimmy called and I accidentally disconnected when I tried to put you on hold."

"Never mind. What happened? Where are they? How are they?"

"They're at the Desert Regional Medical Center. Where are you?"

"I don't know." I looked around. "I just got off the Buzz. I'm somewhere on Palm Canyon Drive, but I'm not sure exactly where."

"I know the Buzz route. Stay where you are, and I'll come get you." She hung up a second time, leaving me no more informed than before.

Rocky and I found a well-populated area filled with wrought-iron tables and chairs. I sat in one and he sat by my foot. Even though we were in public, I was wary of every person who entered my line of vision. Who knew Jimmy and Hudson were going to Salton? Why attack them? Were they the same guys who had approached me at the quarry yesterday? Had the police been notified? How did the men get to the hospital?

I made sure to remain visible from the street so Emma wouldn't have to look hard to spot us. It was hot. My heart was racing from my hasty exit from the trolley. Rocky stretched out the length of his leash and lapped at a bowl of water a local business had left out for such occasions. I couldn't sit still not knowing what was going on, so I called Hudson again.

"Madison," he said. He coughed a few times. "Hey."

"Emma just called me and said you and Jimmy were in the hospital because you got into a fight. What's going on?"

"I guess it's a day of surprises." His voice sounded strained, as if he was having trouble breathing. Emma had said they'd been in a fight, but she hadn't meant a verbal one.

"Where are you?"

"The emergency room." He coughed again. "They're not real fast over here. I might be a little late for our romantic evening."

"Are you okay?"

"I'll survive."

Questions crowded my head, but Hudson's simple answers and forced light tone were making it difficult for me to focus. "What about Jimmy? How's he?"

"Don't know. They took him one direction and sent me another. I can't really talk right now. I'll call you later, okay, hon?"

"Okay," I said, though it was anything but.

Emma pulled up to the curb in front of me twenty-three minutes later. I was near crazy with worry. The top on the convertible was down and her bike rested on the backseat. I moved a pile of blue and white striped beach towels and swim goggles to the back and climbed into her car, buckled the seatbelt, and held Rocky on my lap. She peeled away from the curb fast enough to let me know she wanted to reach the hospital as much as I did.

"I talked to Hudson," I said.

"How is he? Jimmy didn't know."

"He sounded like he was tired or having trouble breathing. How's Jimmy?"

"I don't know. He told me where they were and then said he had to go." She started to cry. Tears streamed down her face, and every few seconds she took her hand off the wheel to brush them off her cheeks.

We lapsed into silence. Emma challenged the speed limit and barely made two yellow lights. The third, which turned red before we entered the intersection, proved to be her undoing. A police car pulled out from the side of the road and tailed us. She ignored his flashing lights, but when he turned on his siren, she pulled over.

I twisted around. The black and white car pulled up behind us and Officer Buchanan got out. He approached the driver's side window.

Emma stared at the wheel, her hands in her lap. She gave up wiping away the tears and they dripped from her face onto her shirt.

"Ms. McKenna, may I have your license and registration?" he asked. She nodded but didn't look at him.

I leaned forward and looked at him through Emma's window. "Officer, we're on our way to the hospital," I said. "Hudson and Jimmy were admitted to the emergency room."

His expression changed. "What happened?"

"We don't know yet," Emma said.

I looked at Emma. Her face had gone pale. It hit me that I'd assumed Jimmy called her, but that didn't seem to be the case. She called him when I called Hudson, and neither had been able to talk. How had she known about the fight? And then I remembered their argument and her storming out of the house.

I put my hand on her forearm in a gesture I hoped conveyed that I sensed her fear. "They headed out to Salton Springs this morning. Emma called me as soon as she heard they had trouble, but we don't know the extent of it. Please—" I said, and then caught myself. There was no point asking for leniency.

Buchanan went back to his car with Emma's license and registration. A few minutes later, he returned. He leaned toward us and put his hands on the top of the car. I could hear his fingers strumming the roof. He looked at Emma for a few seconds and then at me. "I'm not going to give you a ticket as long as you two trade places."

Emma nodded her head but didn't look at either of us. I let go of her forearm and set Rocky on the seat between us. I got out and walked around the back of the car. The officer met me by the trunk. "Mrs. McKenna is clearly very upset. I don't think she should be behind the wheel." I must have looked confused, because he continued. "When I ran your background, I didn't see any traffic violations."

I nodded. The only thing I wanted was to get us to the hospital and find out what happened.

"One last thing," he said. "The hospital isn't going to allow you to take your dog inside. How about I take him to the precinct? You can pick him up when you're done."

The answer was no, but the alternative—leaving Rocky alone in the car in hundred-degree heat—wasn't acceptable either. I searched the officer's face for signs I could trust him with arguably the most important presence in my life. I realized I was being forced to make a choice between Hudson and Rocky and I didn't like how that felt.

"He's everything to me," I said.

"He'll be okay."

Tears sprung to my eyes. "I mean Rocky," I whispered. I braced myself for the officer's judgment.

"When my wife died, I adopted a Pomeranian," he said. "I knew what you meant."

I swiped the tears off my face. It wouldn't do anybody any good for me to cry, not Emma, not Hudson, not Rocky. I went to the driver's side. Emma had slid across the front seat and was buckled in. Her arms were wrapped around Rocky the same way her daughter Heather hugged him. All of a sudden, Emma seemed not like an adult but like a young girl who had done something wrong and was afraid of her punishment.

"Officer Buchanan is going to take Rocky. I'll pick him up when we're done."

She relaxed her arms and Rocky jumped out and ran to me. I picked him up and kissed him. "You have to behave," I said. "I'll pick you up as soon as I can."

Rocky nuzzled my face and then wriggled out of my arms. He ran to a patch of dry desert brush and left behind evidence of his own fear. I handed his leash off to the police officer and climbed into Emma's car feeling all kinds of emptiness.

I parked in a lot identified as visitor parking and Emma was out of the car before I'd put on the emergency brake. I caught up with her and cut off her path before we entered. "Hudson told me they took Jimmy one way and him another. Once we go inside, we're probably not going to see each other. Is there anything you need to tell me? Anything you know about what happened today or—just—anything?"

Her face had gone from the ghostly pale I'd seen in the car to flushed red. She was on the verge of crying again, but was trying hard to hold herself together. She grabbed both of my hands and squeezed them. "Everything happening around here is my fault."

"Emma, this isn't your fault. You weren't anywhere near the guys today. You don't even know what happened. Try to be strong. Two men you love are in there and for all we know, they'll be examined and sent on their way with a bottle of painkillers. Don't jump to conclusions," I said.

But the men wouldn't be sent home with a warning to rest and a bottle of painkillers. Hudson had a mild concussion. Jimmy had a collapsed lung and two cracked ribs. They were both admitted overnight with no immediate plans for release.

# EIGHTEEN

I had more than enough experience with hospitals to make me hate them. My first memory was from the time I tore my ACL while skiing away from the man I thought I'd spend my life with. In twenty-four hours I went from receiving a proclamation of his love to the news he was married, then to two dozen pink and yellow roses delivered with a note that said, "I'm sorry. I need more time." It turned out his personal demons beat out his desire to make it up to me.

My most recent hospital stay had come after the life-threatening fight that caused my nightmares. The physical injuries sustained had been temporary. Hudson had looked after me during those first few weeks. My reliance on sedatives to sleep through the night had approached addiction. The nightmares had started when I stopped taking the pills. The only reason I'd held out on telling Hudson about the pills, the flashbacks, and the nightmares was because I didn't want to take away how much it had meant to know he'd been there for me.

The Desert Regional Medical Center was more architecturally interesting than any of the hospitals I'd stayed at, but the smell was the same. It conjured up thoughts of tongue depressors and cotton swabs with a faint antiseptic cherry overlay. My throat constricted and I forced a dry swallow.

Emma and I were updated on the condition of the men shortly after arriving. A man in white scrubs volunteered to escort Emma to Jimmy's bed. As I had no official relationship to Hudson other than girlfriend (a term that felt far too awkward to use considering my age), I was told to find a seat and wait.

And wait.

And wait.

Two hours passed. The assortment of people in the waiting room thinned out. I exhausted the entertainment factor of my phone and finally went out front to check in on Rocky.

"This is Madison Night," I said when Officer Buchanan answered. "How's Rocky?"

"He's a sweet dog. Kinda changes things around the office. Don't tell anybody, but I took a secret video of some of the guys playing fetch with him. Should be good for the annual holiday party."

I pictured how Tex and Hudson had both been charmed by Rocky. "He has that effect on people," I said.

"How are the men?"

"I don't know details. I don't even know what happened. They told us Jimmy has broken ribs and a collapsed lung and Hudson has a mild concussion. Neither one is getting out tonight. Emma's with Jimmy, but they won't let me back to see Hudson."

"Let me make a phone call. I'll see what I can do."

The officer's offer surprised me, but I wasn't about to question his motivation. "Thank you," I said. A moment passed and then I inquired about his investigation. "Have you determined anything about the body? The identity or the cause of death?"

"The identity hasn't been released yet, but the cause of death was drowning."

"That's horrible." I waited a few moments, expecting him to tell me more. He did not. "I should go back into the waiting room in case they change their mind about Hudson having visitors. I appreciate anything you can do to make that happen."

"I'm on it."

I thanked him again and went back inside. Omar, the same orderly who had attended to my tetanus shot needs, approached me. "Madison, how's the leg?"

"Better. A few more days under a Band-Aid and it'll be good as new."

He chuckled. "Watch out. That Band-Aid is going to leave you with some funny tan lines."

"Good thing I use sunscreen." I looked at the desk where I'd had no luck getting information about Hudson. "Can you help me get an update on a patient?"

"Who?"

"Hudson James. He's the one who brought me the other day."

"Don't tell me he's getting a tetanus shot too. I should have given you the two-for-one special." He smiled.

I tried to match his expression, but my face felt frozen. "Not exactly. He came in a couple of hours ago with another guy. I don't know who brought them or what happened. Nobody will tell me anything."

"Follow me." Omar led me to the nurses' station and said something to the woman behind the counter. She looked at him, then at me, and then at him again, this time nodding. She pointed behind her and Omar looked up at the gray doors. "He's in the ER waiting room. Come on. I'll take you back to see him."

I put my phone in my pocket and followed him. We passed through heavy doors the shade of silly putty. They swung shut behind us. He turned left and then used a small ID card to scan us into a wing not open to the public.

"Crazy thing happened to your friends," Omar said. "There's a rough crowd out by the Salton Sea. They're not known to mess with people during the day, but the way Mr. James told it to the police, it was like they were waiting for them."

"Who?"

"Benji Nalder's gang."

Benji Nalder. Aside from the face-off at the quarry, he was like a ghost at the fringes of our time in Palm Springs. I'd wanted to see the confrontation at the quarry as an isolated incident, but I couldn't, not now. I'd gotten out of there before Benji got physical, but he'd used intimidation tactics to scare me. And now it seemed he and his gang had been responsible for jumping Hudson and Jimmy in Salton, which meant my omission of information could have prevented the attack. I'd been defensive after Jimmy accused me of playing the victim. What had they been doing in the quarry and what did it have to do with the attack on the men today?

Omar continued. "A couple of them have been arrested for possession of drugs, but Benji always manages to stay in the clear. Last year some kids came in here high as a kite, said they bought the stuff from him. They died in the ER. Benji doesn't come around Palm Springs anymore. The cops are so desperate to get something on him they'd probably push him into an intersection and arrest him for jaywalking."

We went through another set of doors. To the left of us was a row of curtained off beds. To the right was a large U-shaped area where several hospital personnel worked. Omar walked to the second curtain on the left and pulled the fabric back. "Mr. James, you have a visitor."

Aside from the backdrop of the hospital bed, the heart monitor machines, and the bleached white linens, Hudson looked much the same as the last time I'd seen him. Instead of a bandana tied over his black hair, it was white gauze. His black T-shirt had been replaced by a hospital gown. There was a small cut over his left eye, held shut with two butterfly bandages, and a bruise on his cheek below. His bottom lip appeared to be slightly fuller than usual. I moved to his side, held my left index finger to my lips, and then transferred a kiss to his. He flinched almost imperceptibly. His tongue flicked out over his bottom lip and I noticed a small cut there as well.

"How are you feeling?" Omar asked Hudson.

"Great. They gave me some painkillers about half an hour ago and I think I'm starting to hallucinate." He looked at me. "I could swear my girlfriend is standing next to the bed."

I took his hand and he ran his thumb back and forth over my fingers.

"If you need anything, press the call button," Omar said.

"Someone should be by to move you in the next hour or so. We're just waiting on an available bed."

Omar left. I pulled a gray plastic chair closer to the bed and sat down. "Do you want to tell me what happened?" I asked.

"I'd rather talk about you," Hudson said. "You sure you're okay?"

I couldn't ignore that Hudson avoided details of his attack in much the same manner I'd avoided telling him about what had happened to me. "You're the one in a hospital bed, not me," I said gently. "Just think, if you hadn't convinced them to keep you overnight, you might have gotten the Florence Nightingale treatment."

"Doris Day never played a nurse," he said.

"Shows what you know. *The Doris Day Show*, season four. She impersonates a nurse on one of the Peter Lawford episodes." I held my hands up to my head. "She wore a cute little hat and everything."

"I should have known." A smile flashed across his face but then disappeared almost immediately. As close as I felt to Hudson, I became aware of the distance between us. He'd been attacked by the same people who had approached me at the quarry. I had to come to terms with the fact that my life wasn't just about me anymore.

"This is not what I had in mind when I asked you to come with me to Palm Springs," he said. He raised his hand to his lip and touched it, and then looked at his fingers as if expecting to see blood. He picked up my hand with his other hand and held it.

"Really?" I said lightly. "And here I thought you were making sure we had an exciting time."

The smile returned to his face if only briefly. "You hear anything about Jimmy?"

"When we got here they told us he had a collapsed lung and you had a concussion. Emma went to see him, but I've been waiting out front."

"They wouldn't let you come back?"

I held my left hand up and pointed to my empty ring finger. "Seems I didn't have the proper credentials."

His voice grew husky. "Do you want the proper credentials?"

"I want you to get better," I said softly.

He nodded his head slightly and then closed his eyes. Whatever medication had eased his pain had pulled him into slumber. I wondered briefly if he'd remember our conversation when he woke up.

I remained by Hudson's bed until they asked me to leave. Plans to move him had been delayed based on another patient. He'd woken up twice, but both times fell back asleep quickly.

I found Emma in the lobby. Her makeup was gone from her face and her puffy eyes indicated where it had gone. She stood up when she saw me. I put my arm around her and guided her out of the ER to the car. There was no discussion over who would drive.

The main roads of Palm Springs were becoming more familiar to me, but the roundabout way we'd reached the hospital had put me off my compass. Emma navigated with the occasional, "left here," and "right at the light." Before long we entered the stretch of dirt road that led to her and Jimmy's house.

I pulled into the driveway. "Emma, you and Heather shouldn't stay here by yourselves tonight. Go inside and pack overnight bags. I'll get Mortiboy. Tell Heather we're going to have our own sleepover. We can all stay in my motel room. I'll call Officer Buchanan and ask him to meet us there with Rocky."

Emma nodded. The life had been sucked from her and the only thing she was capable of was following instructions. She went inside the house and I called Buchanan.

"Hi, Officer. It's Madison Night. Thank you again for getting me in to see Hudson. I've been with him most of the day, but they just kicked us out."

"Glad I could help."

"I was wondering if we could arrange for me to pick up Rocky."

"Sure. I'm just finishing up with the ME. Are you still at the hospital?"

"We're at Emma's house, but we're going from here to the Tiki Tropics motel. Why don't I call you when we're there?"

"Sounds good."

At that moment, Emma ran out of the house with a half-filled suitcase in one hand and her phone in the other. Her eyes looked wild. She dropped the suitcase and ran to me.

"Madison, the school called to make sure Heather got home safely. She's not here. Nobody's here. I don't know what to do." She held up the phone. "My little girl is missing!"

# NINETEEN

I took the phone from Emma's hand. "Hello?" I asked. "Who is this?"

"Madison? It's Jo Conway. Emma called me. Is everything okay?"

"I don't think so. Can you hold on for a moment?" I set the phone down on the end table and led Emma to the sofa. She sat down and bent over, gasping for breath. "What did the school tell you?"

"They said they gave Heather the message that I was running late. The vice principal said Heather waited on the steps, but she was gone when he left. He wanted to check to make sure everything was okay."

"Did you call the school?"

"No. I was with you at the hospital. I left a message for Jo—"

Despite the desert heat, I felt chilled. I became vaguely aware of a tinny sound and it took me a second to realize Jo was still on the phone. "Wait here." I picked up the phone and went into the next room. "Jo? Are you still there?"

"Yes. What's wrong?"

"Did you see Heather when you picked Gina up from school today?"

"No, but I took Gina out of class early today, so I wasn't there at the usual time."

"Did you get a message from Emma?"

"No. Why? What is going on?"

"Heather's missing. I have to call the police."

I hung up and called Buchanan. "Officer, this is Madison Night. Emma's little girl is missing."

"For how long?"

"There was a mix-up at the school, so it's been a couple of hours."

"Tell Ms. McKenna to call the school and anybody else Heather might be with. It's too soon for official action."

"But she's nine years old! Isn't there anything you can do?"

He was quiet for a moment, and then said, "I'm on my way."

The day that wouldn't end got even longer. Emma called the school, the teachers, and the last five babysitters she'd hired to sit Heather. I went next door and checked to see if Jo was home. None of our actions netted us answers.

What had happened while we'd been at the hospital? The details were thin. Someone had called the school and posed as Emma. They'd left a nine-year-old girl vulnerable and alone and now she was missing. Someone had known we'd be gone all day, someone who'd been responsible for Hudson and Jimmy's injuries. It sickened me further to think the assault on the men had been little more than a diversionary tactic.

While my mind backtracked over everything that had happened since arriving in Palm Springs, Emma sat next to me, as still as a statue except for the action of chipping off her nail polish.

Buchanan arrived in minutes. He let Rocky out of the car, and he ran to me, his fur flying behind him. Emma stood up. "Have you found her?"

"I'm sorry, Ms. McKenna, like I told Ms. Night, it's too soon for us to take any official action."

"But my little girl is gone!" She was borderline hysterical. I hugged Rocky to my chest and thought about the alternative, how I'd feel if it had been him.

"Officer, there must be something you can do," I said. I set Rocky down on the yard and held tightly to his leash.

"Tell me what you know," he said.

Emma wiped the tears from her face. "Her school lets out at

two. The school claims I called them and said I was running late and asked Heather to wait out front for me—but I didn't. The vice principal said when he left, Heather wasn't there anymore, so he thought I picked her up. He called here to make sure everything was okay—that's how I found out she never came home."

Buchanan looked uncomfortable. He shifted his weight from one foot to the other, and then tapped his right foot against the step a few times like I did when I felt mine going numb.

"Officer, where were you when we called?"

"At the station house. I was about to take your dog to my house where my Pomeranian is, but two dogs that don't know each other...not a good idea. I asked one of the patrol officers to watch him while I met with the ME. That's when I got your call."

"But you're a patrol officer too, right? Why are you involved in this case?"

"I feel a little to blame for this investigation getting messed up from the start and I want to help Detective Drayton see it through." Buchanan turned his attention to Emma. "Mrs. McKenna, I'd like to take a look in the house, see if anything is amiss."

Emma didn't have to let him inside, but unless she was hiding something, there was no reason not to. No matter what guilt she felt over her affair, it had been pushed aside to make room for the protection mode she needed to find her daughter. We both stood up. She opened the front door and led the three of us inside.

The house looked much like it had when I'd left that morning. Jimmy's coffee mug, plate, and fork sat in the sink. A bag of bagels sat on the counter. A bowl of water sat on the floor.

"Mortiboy," I said. The three of them looked at me. "Hudson's cat. He should be here somewhere."

"What does this cat look like?"

"He's black, probably about five or six years old."

"Would he come if you called him?"

"If Hudson called him, maybe. Not me. He still associates me with my dog, and they aren't the best of friends."

"Takes time with cats, especially ones who are used to living on their own. Mine's had four years to get used to having a Pomeranian's nose in her butt and she still hasn't accepted it," Buchanan said.

We moved through the house in a group, though no doubt we were all looking for something different. I kept my eyes out for Mortiboy. With Hudson recovering in the hospital, the last thing he'd want to hear was that somehow I'd lost his cat.

Emma moved Jimmy's dishes into the dishwasher, hung the dish towel on the hook by the refrigerator, and tucked the bag of bagels into the cabinet. In the bathroom she moved the towel from over the shower curtain rod to the hook on the back of the door, and scooped up jeans, T-shirt, and men's boxer shorts from a pile on the floor. She tossed the clothes into the open wicker hamper, only to be rewarded with an annoyed meow. We all peered in at Mortiboy, half buried under dirty garments.

I reached in and lifted him out. He wriggled from my arms and jumped onto the floor, and then stalked out of the bathroom down the hallway into the kitchen. He lowered his head over the water bowl and lapped it up.

"Mrs. McKenna, do you see anything out of the ordinary? Anything missing, moved?"

"No. The house looks exactly as I left it." She looked at me and I nodded.

"It looks the same as it did this morning to me too except for the bagels, but Hudson was out getting them when I left."

"What time was that?"

I shrugged and bounced the toe of my lilac sneaker against the linoleum floor. "Around nine, I think? I overslept this morning and got a late start."

Buchanan made a note. My cell phone rang. I didn't recognize the number.

"Hello?"

"Is this Madison Night?" asked a female voice.

"Yes, who is this?"

"Lora. From the park. You left your name and number when

you found a set of keys by the pier?" Her voice rose in a question as if to jog my memory.

"Oh. Yes. Hi." I said "excuse me" to Buchanan and Emma. "I'm sorry. We have a—a situation here. I don't really care if anybody claimed those keys."

"I'm not calling about the keys."

"But you said—"

"I'm calling about a little girl who says she knows you. Her name is Heather?"

"Do you know where she is?" I asked.

Both Buchanan and Emma turned to face me. Emma raced forward and put her hands on my arms. Her eyes were wide. "Where is she?" she asked. "Is she okay?"

I held up my finger.

"Lora, is Heather with you? Is she okay?"

"She's okay, but she's scared. I don't know how she got here. She said she was waiting for her mom to come pick her up. It's time for me to close the gates, but I didn't feel right leaving her here. I can bring her home if you give me the address."

I tipped my head back and closed my eyes. Relief washed over me. I dropped into a kitchen chair. "She's at the park with one of the rangers," I said to Emma.

Emma snatched the phone from my hand. She put her left hand over her left ear and held the phone to her right. "Let me talk to her," she said. "Heather? Honey, is that you?" After a slight pause, she dropped down, knees first, directly onto the kitchen floor. "I'll be right there. I promise. I love you." She hung up and grabbed her keys. "I'm going to the park," she said.

"I still think you and Heather should come to the motel and stay with me." I said. "None of us should be alone. Not tonight."

Emma put up less of an argument than I might have if our positions were reversed, which only added to my suspicions there was more going on under the surface than I knew.

"Sounds to me like this is a big mix-up," Buchanan said. He smiled, as though everything had gone back to normal. But as we made our way back down the hallway, it occurred to me that Lora from Parks and Recreation might not be as uninvolved as she seemed.

# TWENTY

Lora had been at the park the day I turned in the keys, but so had Benji. I had distinctly gotten the feeling that they knew one another. That had been the day Benji and his pals approached me in the quarry, and later that same day the body had been found. Was it possible that Lora, in her role as park ranger, helped orchestrate the murder by the river?

I needed to talk things out. Twice Emma had claimed credit or blame for the events unfolding around us, but as far as I could see, there were other players. I was glad that Buchanan offered to take Emma to the park, but I suspected that even though he was acting in an unofficial manner, he wanted to make sure Heather was okay. None of us believed this was a communication mix-up. It had to do with the murder of Dr. Albert Hall. I didn't believe Emma to be capable of murder, but I sensed there was more to her story than she'd told me.

I stayed behind and packed after Emma and Buchanan left. The guest room looked bigger now that my turquoise Samsonite luggage was gone. Hudson, being of a generally neat disposition, had unpacked when we arrived. Aside from the suitcase in the corner, there was barely any evidence the room was in use.

I retrieved Mortiboy from the hamper (he'd climbed back in) and eased him into his carrier. The clock ticked by while I sat in the living room, waiting for them to return. I stared at the screen of my phone for a few seconds, and then called the most recent number.

"Lora, this is Madison Night."

"Hi. Emma and that policeman were just here."

"So Heather is okay?"

"She's okay. She's better than okay. She's a good kid."

"What can you tell me about this afternoon?"

"The same thing I told Officer Buchanan, which is not much. I check the public restrooms at three o'clock every day. The park was empty when I went in, but when I came out, Heather was sitting at a picnic table doing her homework."

"Just like that? No signs of where she came from or who brought her?"

"She was all alone. I kept an eye on her from a distance, but after about ten minutes something seemed off. I sat down with her and asked her how she got there."

"And?"

"She said she got a message to meet her mom at the park. It's only a couple of blocks from the school so she walked."

"Who gave her this message?"

"I don't know. Somebody at the school, I think."

Emma was going to be furious. I would be. And the more I thought about it, the more suspicious it all became. I didn't trust Lora, but then again, if she wasn't to be trusted, why had she called and told us Heather was there? Why was she showing no signs of fear at talking to the police?

"Lora, there was a man at the park the day I dropped off the keys. Tall and thin. I got the feeling you knew him."

"A lot of people come through the park."

"This one was different. After I left you, I went to the quarry and he threatened me."

"Did you tell the police?"

"Yes."

"I'm sure they'll take care of it."

"Why did you call me?" I asked suddenly. "Why not Heather's mom? Heather must know the number."

"I tried to call her mom, but there was no answer. I asked Heather if she had any other family or if there was someone else I could call and she said you. I remembered that you left your phone number here. I wish I could help more," Lora said.

My phone beeped with an incoming call. It was Emma. "I have another call coming in. Are you sure there's nothing else you want to tell me?" I asked. She was silent. "I have to go."

Emma's call was brief. Heather was okay and they were on their way to the Tiki Tropics. I promised to pack pajamas for everyone and meet them in a few minutes. I was in the process of dragging suitcases and animals out of the house when Jo pulled into her driveway.

She came over to help. "What happened today? Emma sounded hysterical on the phone."

"She was." Considering my suspicions about the day's events, I didn't think it was my place to put Emma's parenting skills in a poor light. "There was a mix-up at the school and Heather ended up waiting for her in the wrong place."

"But she's okay now?"

"She is. Emma and Heather are meeting me at the Tiki motel."

"What about the guys?"

"Long story." I smiled. "You haven't seen any strangers in the neighborhood recently, have you?"

"The only strangers are you and Hudson. Why?"

"Just curious."

"I doubt I'd be any help even if there were. When I'm at home, I tend to be in the zone. The studio," she added by way of explanation. "The orchestra gave me a new arrangement. Once I get Gina started on her homework I put on the headphones and listen to it on repeat. It's my way of feeling the music. Everybody has their process. That's mine." She studied me. "You and Hudson aren't leaving soon, are you?"

"No. Why?"

"I'll try to get the four of you tickets to the concert."

"Sounds great."

We fit the suitcases into the trunk of the car and I eased Mortiboy's carrier onto the backseat. Jo scooped up Rocky and stroked his fur. "This hasn't been a particularly relaxing trip for you, has it?" Jo asked me.

"It's been an unusual couple of days," I said. I took Rocky and set him on the front seat. "If you don't have any plans tonight, you and Gina should join us for a girls' night in at the motel."

"Thanks for the offer, but I've got a real rehearsal tonight. Too bad. It sounds like fun."

I drove to the motel. Emma and Heather were waiting for me in the lobby when I arrived. Heather was dressed in her school clothes: a pink top featuring Jem and the Holograms, jeans, and formerly white sneakers that were coated with a layer of dry dirt. Her fair blonde hair was in ponytails that were slightly lopsided. She looked up at me with wide eyes and I stooped down and hugged her. When she let go, I handed Rocky's leash over to her and carried Mortiboy's carrier myself.

The room was on the second floor. When we were inside, I let Mortiboy out of his cage and then unclipped Rocky's leash. He ran to the bed and yapped at Mortiboy. Heather smiled. Emma changed into her pajamas while I went to the bathroom and took my turn in the shower. When I was done, I found Rocky, Mortiboy, and Heather playing on the bed.

"You had a big day today, didn't you?" I asked Heather.

She ran her open hand over Rocky's fur and nodded. "I wasn't scared," she said bravely, though her otherwise quiet disposition spoke otherwise. "The ranger lady kept me company."

"That was nice of her. What did you talk about?"

"She asked me if I had any brothers or sisters. She has a big brother. She said I was lucky that I didn't."

I laughed. "A lot of people feel that way."

"Uncle Hudson is my mom's brother and she doesn't feel that way," she said.

"That's true, but your Uncle Hudson is one in a million."

"A million is a lot," she said after careful consideration. "If those are the odds then I guess I am lucky."

I left Heather on the bed with the animals and joined Emma

on the balcony. She held an almost empty glass of wine. I poured one for myself and refilled hers. We stood side by side and looked down at the pool. Only a few people remained on the deck, absorbing the last rays of the hot sun. The air was a mixture of coconuts and chlorine. As a lifelong devotee of sunscreen SPF 50+, I could never smell the scent of coconuts and not think of the kind of deeply bronzed skin I'd never once had the abandon to pursue. Emma was attentive to Heather in a way that spoke volumes about her earlier fears. Eventually she joined me on the balcony. "I put my daughter's life at risk. I don't know how it got to this."

"Heather's going to be okay now, but how are you?"

"Shaken up," she said. She set her glass down and stared out at the palm trees surrounding the pool in front of us.

"Am I a bad wife because I didn't ask to spend the night at the hospital?" she asked.

"If Jimmy is on painkillers, he probably wouldn't even know if you were there."

"What have I done to my life?" she asked quietly. "I broke my marriage vows and put Heather in danger, for what?" Tears trickled out of her eyes and down her cheeks. She swiped them away and patted her fingertips on her jeans.

"You're here, taking care of Heather now. Jimmy would appreciate that. Do you want to talk about how it all started?" I asked softly.

She pulled her feet up under her. "It sounds like such a cliché. Married woman has an affair with her therapist. But it wasn't like that. I didn't even know he was a doctor when we met."

"How *did* you meet?"

"At the antique marketplace. I was looking for some baskets for the house, you know, Moroccan style. I saw the idea in a magazine. I thought maybe if I redecorated, made the house more exotic, it would be, I don't know, a change. Jimmy and I were in a rut. It's not like we could take off for a vacation, not with Heather in school." We turned around and looked in the room at Heather. She held Mortiboy on her lap while Rocky looked on from a foot away.

It was unclear how she'd gotten Mortiboy to accept such human-to-cat affection. I'd certainly never broken through to that level. "So I got this crazy idea I could redecorate. Maybe we'd do it together and it would give us something to focus on."

"How did a plan to bring your family closer together lead to your affair?" I asked.

Emma laughed. "You don't do this girlfriends-sharing-secrets thing very often, do you?" she asked. As horrified as I was, it seemed my inappropriate question had shattered some kind of barrier between us. Emma relaxed noticeably.

She was right. I didn't have a lot of experience with the girlfriend conversation thing. When the rug had been pulled out from underneath the relationship I'd been in before fleeing to Texas, I questioned everything I'd thought was real. My own circle of friends was scattered around the country: Susan, the film distributor in Hollywood who helped me obtain movie prints for the theater where I volunteered; Joannie, the owner of Joannie Loves Tchotchkes, a thrift shop in Lakewood who often beat me to estate sales and then profited when she sold me items of interest; and Connie, half of a hipster couple who had hired me to redecorate their kitchen. I almost laughed out loud when I thought of former police officer Donna Nast. She was the anti-me in so many ways, yet thanks to horrific circumstances, we'd been forced to put our differences aside and cooperate with each other.

Nasty and I would never be friends. Emma and I could.

"Okay, do-over. Tell me about how it started."

She smiled and stared off at a vague spot above the pool. "Albert was at the booth with the baskets too. I picked out a few that I liked, but didn't think about how I was going to get them to the car. He offered to help me, so I went a little crazy and bought a bunch. We probably looked pretty funny, balancing stacks of these woven baskets on our heads." She held her hands up to the space on either side of her head, and then laughed at the memory. "It was the easiest way to carry them. It wasn't until we filled both of our cars that I noticed his white shirt was stained with some kind of clay-colored dirt. I offered to pay for the dry cleaning but he said no, it would come clean with soap and water. He followed me home with his car full of baskets and that was supposed to be that."

"Where was Jimmy?"

"Out at the quarry, not that it mattered. Albert helped me with the baskets and asked if he could use my bathroom to try to clean his shirt. When he came out, it was wet and the stain was worse. I offered to run it through the washing machine."

"So that's when it started?"

"No, it wasn't like that. He followed me home, I washed his shirt, and he left. When we said goodbye, he said he hoped he'd run into me again sometime and wished me luck with the redecorating. It was totally innocent."

I refilled both of our glasses, Emma's a little more than mine. I wanted her to keep talking, and I wanted to remember everything she said. Nothing I knew connected back to what had happened to Hudson and Jimmy, but it connected to Albert Hall, and that was enough. I didn't believe much in coincidence. Not anymore.

Emma picked up her glass and took a sizeable swallow. She set it down again and then ran both of her hands through her hair, pulling it back off her face and into a makeshift ponytail. "A strange man helped me out. It should have stopped there. But I liked the attention. I liked that he flirted with me at the antique fair. I told myself I was doing nothing wrong because I'd told him about Jimmy and Heather right away. But I went back to the fair the next week hoping to see him. I even dressed up a little bit. One of those full-skirted dresses like you wear and sandals that laced up my legs."

"Was he there?"

She nodded. "Same booth. The Moroccan baskets. He said he hadn't had a chance to buy what he wanted because he'd left early to help me. I said it was only right for me to help him this time, and that's how we ended up back at his place."

It was my turn to nod. Another woman might have told Emma when she got married, she made a promise not to act on those feelings, but I wouldn't. My own romantic history included a married man. Had he been there for me after he confessed, after I skied away from him and gotten into the accident that permanently injured my knee, had he indicated he still wanted me in his life, I knew I would have agreed. Nothing about that memory was good: not what had happened, not what I'd learned about myself when it happened, not how I'd grown as a person after it was over. But no matter what, I lived with the knowledge that I'd once been open to love, and after Brad, I'd been forever changed. Years had passed and I was only starting to accept romance back into my life. Whatever was between Emma and Jimmy was something nobody else would fully understand, but it wasn't my place to judge.

I looked up at Emma. She'd been quiet for a few seconds, but started talking again. "He invited me to stay for lunch and I said yes. We had quesadillas and salsa and I got a little on my dress. He said he'd wash it for me, just like I did for him—and instead of laughing it off, I reached around to my back and undid my zipper and let my dress fall to the living-room floor."

Oh, my.

Emma finished her third glass of wine and her voice dropped to a whisper. "I don't regret it. Sometimes Jimmy isn't a very nice person. Sometimes he drinks a lot and doesn't treat me well. And Albert was a nice, attractive man who treated me like a princess. And he didn't have a wedding ring, so I assumed the only one risking anything was me. I know it was wrong, but I'm still glad I did it. Does that make me horrible?"

"What you did doesn't make you a horrible person, it makes you a real person."

"Madison, when I came to Dallas to see Hudson last year, that wasn't a regular visit. Jimmy and I needed a break. A separation. But we don't have enough money for me to move out. Jimmy makes the money while I take care of Heather, so I had nowhere to go. After what happened with Hudson, when his past came up, I asked if he wanted to come stay with us. He did, and it helped a little, but I knew sooner or later he was going back. He kept saying there was something in Dallas he wasn't willing to leave behind. Now I know he meant you."

"Was Hudson always like he is now?"

"If you're asking about his love life, I can't tell you too much. Hudson was always a private guy. When he had a girlfriend, it was just her. He didn't juggle or date around."

I looked down at my glass. "Anybody serious?"

"Sure," she said. "By the time you're our age, we've all had somebody serious in our past. But that was a long time ago. A lot of people shut him out when he was suspected of murder. Or maybe he shut them out first—I don't know. But as far as I know, you're the only one he's opened up to since then."

Whether it was the wine or the candid girl talk or a combination of the two, I didn't know, but this time it was me who struggled to hold back tears. When Hudson's reputation had been cleared, the circumstances had shifted our relationship from landlord/handyman to something more personal, and when it was over, he'd let me know he wanted more. I hadn't been ready. Hudson had packed up his truck and left town, leaving me to wonder if I'd let something good slip through my fingertips because I wasn't able to get past my own emotional prison.

He'd told me he visited his sister, but had never mentioned anything more. Had he known about their marital problems? Had he accepted the role of intermediary in order to help Emma, or had he been playing protective big brother, making sure Jimmy didn't put her or Heather at risk? And when Emma had brought Heather to Dallas earlier in the year, had that really been just a family vacation, or had Hudson been trying in his own way to offer her the same getaway she'd offered him?

I reached my hand out and squeezed Emma's. "Sometimes life doesn't turn out the way you think it will," I said. "None of us know anything. We're all just trying to do what we can to be happy and not hurt anybody else."

"Madison, there's something I haven't told you," she said quietly. She stared into the bottom of her empty wineglass.

What else could there possibly be?

"The day you arrived, the accident where you and Hudson were driven off the road. The car—the SUV—was Albert." She looked down at her hands and spun her gold wedding ring around her finger a couple of times. "That's the day I found out he used to be married to my neighbor, Jo."

I'd started wondering about that. The girls were friends. The mothers were friends. But Jo had moved into the house next door to Jimmy and Emma after the divorce, and she appeared to have no regrets about the dissolution of her union with the doctor.

"I was next door with her," Emma continued. "The girls wanted to bake cookies together, so we made an afternoon of it. Jimmy was getting the food for the cookout."

Rocky shifted his weight against my foot and let out a puff of air. "What happened next?" I prompted.

"Hudson called me when your plane landed. Even though it would have taken time for you to get from the airport to here, I started watching the window. Excited about your visit, I guess."

"We were excited too. The ride from the airport felt like the longest ride in the world."

She smiled, but it was bittersweet. "That truck pulled into the driveway. I knew Jimmy arranged for you to have a Jeep from his fleet, so I was curious. When I saw Albert, I panicked."

"Did Jo see him?"

"Yes, she saw him out the window and called him a dumbass. Said if he was so stupid that he didn't remember which house she lived in, she wasn't going to correct him. She took the girls to the next room so he wouldn't see them through the window. He pounded on my front door for a while and then got into his truck and drove off."

"But he wasn't there to see her, was he? He was there to see you."

"I thought he was there for me. I dumped the milk when Jo wasn't looking and told her I had to go to my house to get more. But when I got there, I called Albert and told him it was over."

"I know it's hard to accept, but you did the right thing. Whatever relationship you had with him was built on an illusion. It wasn't real life. As hard as it is to see now, this is all for the best."

"No, you don't understand. Albert said he understood why I had to break things off, but that he needed to get into my house because he left something behind the last time he was there. So I left the key under the mat and told him to let himself in. I went back to Jo's house to make sure she didn't figure anything out."

"Do you know what it was that he left behind?"

"No," she said. "I thought he meant a sock or a pair of underwear." She blushed. "Something that might come back to haunt me. But now, after what happened that day, I've been over it in my mind a hundred times since then and the only thing I can think is that he was using me for something illegal."

# TWENTY-ONE

"Did you say anything to him?" I asked.

"I didn't know how to confront him without Jo finding out, and I don't know what I would have said to him if I did. I thought about texting him, but my hands were covered in flour and cookie batter."

"Your hands?"

"The cookie making process got a little messy by the third batch." She held her hands out in front of her and inspected her fingernails as if expecting to find cookie dough residue still there.

"How long was he inside?"

"Maybe ten minutes? He came out between the third and fourth batches of cookies. He had two full duffel bags with him that he threw onto the passenger seat of his truck and then he left."

"He must have left in a hurry so he wouldn't get caught."

She nodded. "A couple of minutes after he left you came to my front door. You know the rest."

A slight breeze rearranged the leaves of the palm trees in front of us. Emma tried, unsuccessfully, to stifle a yawn. I didn't know what time it was, but no matter how I looked at it, it had been a particularly long day. There was too much to process. The best thing for all of us was to try to get some sleep.

I carried the empty bottle of wine and the dirty glasses into the room, disposed of the former and rinsed out the latter. Emma crawled into her queen-sized bed next to Heather and Rocky jumped on the other bed, looking at me expectantly. I untucked the sheet and then crawled underneath and let Rocky curl up next to me. The last thing I thought before falling asleep was if Emma was right about Albert using her, and if so, for what.

It was a fitful night of sleep filled with fragmented images of prescription bottles, dirty SUVs, and swirling red and blue lights. Three different times I relived the experience of the Jeep flipping over and Hudson being trapped inside. Three different times I'd woken up before having a chance to go for help. The silver lining was the fact that the recent nightmares triggered from my PTSD had been nowhere in sight.

The next morning, without waking Emma or Heather, I dressed in my bathing suit and grabbed a towel, swim cap, and goggles and then led Rocky out of the room to the pool.

Several years ago I'd discovered the therapeutic aspects of morning swims. Through all of the twists and turns my life had taken over the past few years, swimming had remained a constant, far more effective at restoring calm to my life than any medication might. I believed the cure was in the illness. When I was ready to confront what I'd been through, I'd start to accept it and move on. It was yet another form of self-sufficiency.

The motel pool was shorter than the regulation lap pools I swam in at home, so instead of concentrating on laps swum, I let my mind wander. I'd been in Palm Springs for all of four days, and already I longed for my life back in Dallas. The simplicity of taking a decorating job with Mad for Mod, of getting up early and scouting flea markets, thrift stores, and estate sales. The morbid yet effective practice of combing through the obituaries to learn of recently deceased women of a certain age who might leave behind mid-century marvels. Sketching out room concepts, combing through *Atomic Ranch* magazine, reading posts on RetroRenovation.com, and brainstorming new ways to find clients who appreciated the niche services I offered. Now that summer was behind us, my showroom would be rearranged from the Tiki and Polynesian scene that fit so well with the motel I was staying at to something more cozy. Maybe a Rat Pack era bar or a sunken living room pit with thick white faux fur throw rugs and turquoise furniture. Even though Dallas in September was still pretty hot, the residents, by mutual agreement, chose to crank the AC and pretend it was fall. That was possibly my favorite part of the Dallas culture: the fact residents could pretend the city was whatever they wanted it to be.

Every couple of laps I stopped and checked on the status of Rocky. His leash was looped over the arm of a lounge chair, and he sat underneath it and watched me with his chin flat against the pool deck. The sun was already starting to heat things up. The tension in my body was just about gone after forty-five minutes in the water.

I stopped at the edge of the pool and propped my arms on the deck. "Hey, Rocky, you hanging in there?" I asked him. He lifted his head and looked at me, and then stood up and walked toward the pool. I expected his leash to stop him on his way to the water, but it didn't. It trailed behind him, untethered to anything. Slowly he advanced toward me until he was at the edge. The next thing I knew, he jumped into the water!

The pool was only about three feet deep in the area where I was, so I hopped along the bottom and scooped him up. He wriggled around a bit, and then dog-paddled to the side of the pool. In an awkward display of pet ownership, I picked him up and set him on the deck. He shook his body rapidly, spraying water across the deck. I hoisted myself out of the water and grabbed the end of his leash before it caught on something. I'd taken great care to secure it to the arm of the chaise before I started swimming. How had he gotten loose? I walked him to the chaise and inspected the chair, expecting to find a broken or loose component. The chair was in perfect working order.

I picked up my towel. As the folds of the terrycloth fell open, a small piece of paper fell out and Rocky sniffed it. I picked the paper up and held it open with my thumb and index finger of one hand while I pressed the towel against me with my other. The handwriting inside was the kind of neat cursive scroll no longer taught in elementary schools.

*It's best you start forgetting what you know.*

# TWENTY-TWO

I looked around the pool for signs I wasn't alone. A young black teenager in bright blue swim trunks sauntered in, swinging a whistle around his right hand while he flipped through screens on his cell phone with his left. He made it from the motel lobby to the lifeguard station without looking up. He glanced at the laminated schedule taped to the guard chair and then let it slip through his fingers and continued on.

Other than him, it was me and Rocky.

Until this moment, I'd thought of myself as the person who knew a whole bunch of different bits of information about Albert Hall. Facts that hadn't yet been released, connections between the victim and various people around town, secret affairs and grudges, all things I'd come to learn simply because others had confided in me. With the identity of the victim not yet released to the public, anything I could have reported to the police would have been hearsay, and after the way they'd treated me when I first reported the body, I wasn't willing to go out on that limb again.

But this note changed everything. It meant someone knew what I knew. Someone was watching me. Someone could get to me when I least expected it—here, at the motel, where I had come to get away. Where I thought I'd be safe. How many people even knew I was here?

The thought stopped me mid-towel-off. I looked up at the balcony where Emma and I had sat last night swapping stories and drinking wine. She had as many reasons to want to scare me into silence as anybody else, and she could have easily fed the note between the folds of my towel in the room before I even left.

Then there was Jo Conway. She knew I was staying here. She was the one who had originally given me a ride to the motel—not just the ride, but she'd been the one to suggest it.

The towel had come from Emma and Jimmy's house, and I couldn't rule out Jimmy as having slipped the note into the towel when we were there. He'd been the one to send me to the quarry all alone. He'd even told Hudson to check on me. Had he known Benji would be there? Had he set up the whole thing to scare me?

It was no secret I enjoyed morning swims. Emma had packed the towels from the house. Jimmy could have hidden the note in a towel at the house yesterday or the day before. I would have found it eventually. But untethering Rocky—that had to be done in person, and Jimmy was in the hospital. He might have planted the note, but something else was at play this morning.

And then there was Benji. My encounter with him at the quarry had left me unsettled. He'd attacked Jimmy and Hudson in Salton, but I didn't know why. I'd written him off as a local thug who had wanted to scare me, but what if there was more to his presence?

I stepped into a vintage yellow terrycloth all-in-one shorts suit with a hood and zipped it up over my bathing suit. My wet hair hung down the back, dripping directly into the hood. I slipped on white flip flops with daisies attached to the straps, slung my towel around my shoulders, and gathered Rocky's leash. We walked toward the lifeguard. He stood by the end of the pool, skimming leaves from the water with what appeared to be a strainer on a very long pole.

"Hi," I said. "I'm Madison and this is my dog, Rocky."

"Hey," he said. He glanced at me and Rocky, and then back at the pool.

"You didn't happen to see anybody walking around the pool while I was swimming my laps, did you?"

"Why?"

He pulled the strainer out of the water and held it by his side like Zeus holding a staff.

"I came down early and I had my dog's leash secured to the arm of a chair. When I was done, he wasn't tethered anymore and I think someone let him loose. I was wondering if maybe you saw who did it."

"Which chaise?"

I turned and pointed to the orange and white striped chair at the end of the pool. "The one on the end."

"Yeah, those chairs are old. The leash probably wasn't secure when you started swimming."

"It was."

He shrugged. "You probably thought it was, but it wasn't."

I glared at him for a few seconds. It was clear he didn't believe me, and arguing the point wasn't going to get me anywhere. "Did you see anybody?"

"My shift doesn't start for another ten minutes," he said. "My dad dropped me off early so he could get to work, but it's not my job to look after your dog or your swimming. Not until seven thirty."

I didn't like his attitude. He probably didn't like mine either. "Is it possible for someone to get to the pool if they aren't staying at the motel?" I asked.

"Listen, ma'am, if you have some kind of complaint, you need to take it up with the manager. The pool is open to residents twenty-four seven, but the motel only has a lifeguard on duty from seven thirty to ten. Anything outside of that is your own responsibility. Maybe if you're so worried about your dog, you should have left him in the room."

"What's your name?" I asked.

He appeared stunned by the question. "Why?"

"I'm going to take your suggestion of talking to the motel management, and I think it's a good idea to know which of his employees I talked to this morning."

"Tommy."

"Okay, Tommy, thank you."

I left him on the pool deck and Rocky and I walked back to our room. Emma was still in bed.

"Mmmmmmmm," she said. She stretched her arms over her head and then rubbed her eyes with balled-up fists. Heather was curled up next to her snoring slightly. "Where'd you go?"

"Morning swim."

"You're a better person than I am," she said. "I never get to sleep in anymore."

"Tell you what. Stay in bed as long as you want. I'm going to shower and get dressed, and then I'll go get us some breakfast."

"You're a saint," she said. "I'll be sure to tell my brother." A few seconds later, she was sleeping as soundly as her daughter.


The Tiki Tropics motel had an advertised continental breakfast for guests. I admit I checked it out, hoping for something better than the prepackaged cheese Danishes and Pop-Tarts on display in front of me. I'd taken Emma's keys when I left the room and headed toward the motel lobby to find out my options for food.

The desk manager was a man in his mid-sixties in a brightly printed Hawaiian shirt and light khaki shorts. His white hair was cropped close to his head in a manner that made me think Marines.

"Good morning," he said. "You were up and at 'em early, weren't you?" When I nodded, he continued. "We don't get a lot of early birds here when it's not the tourist season. Kids, they like to get up early. Business folks have to, but the conventions usually start around ten. Party people sometimes come in the off season, but they need their mornings to sleep off the night before. You don't seem to fit any of those categories."

"Option D: None of the above," I offered. He laughed. "I'm here mostly for a getaway, but also a job."

He took in today's ensemble: a pink pullover with a gingham self-belt and matching pink gingham pants (McCalls #5011). Yellow straw hat with a bow in the back. Yellow Keds.

"You sure don't look the corporate type."

It was my turn to laugh. "I'm a decorator. I specialize in mid-century—"

"Ah, that makes a lot more sense," he said. "We've got a lot of that around here. Some people call us the mid-century capital of the world. You live in Los Angeles?"

"No, Dallas, Texas."

"Somebody hired you from Dallas? Seems like a long way to travel to put up some wallpaper in a hundred-degree heat."

"It's a little more involved than wallpaper," I said. "My colleague has some family out here, so we thought two birds, one stone."

He nodded toward the elevator. "Your friend with the little girl, is she your colleague?"

Everything about the man said "chatty motel manager," but something made me aware of the amount of information I was casually offering him. Instead of the full truth, I edited. "She's a friend," I said.

"I've seen her here before with her husband. Nice couple. They stuck to themselves, never complained. Never knew she had a kid though."

I changed the subject. "I'm heading out to get us some breakfast. Can you point me in the direction of a bagel store?"

He glanced at the coffee pots and basket of sugary pastries and then back at me. "Sure. Turn right outside of the parking lot and go about a quarter mile and then turn right again. A couple of miles down the road, you'll get to a strip mall. Got all kinds of options."

"Thank you."

He reached for something on the desk and pulled out a parking permit. "Can't help noticing you came in the metallic green convertible last night. Put this on your dash so the staff knows you're staying here. Not saying we're overbooked or anything, but makes things easier for everybody."

"Sure." I took the parking pass and nudged Rocky to stand up and head toward the door.

"Hey, that's a cute little pooch you got there," he said. "Is he the little fella who caused all the trouble at the pool this morning?"

"What trouble?"

"Tommy, my lifeguard, said a lady claimed somebody broke into the pool and untied her dog while she was swimming. That must have been you."

"It was, but I didn't say someone broke in," I said. I thought back over the conversation with Tommy. "Rocky's leash got loose, and I asked Tommy if he'd seen anybody around, that's all."

"He probably thought you were accusing him. A couple of months ago he forgot to lock the gate and some of his friends had a late-night party. They didn't do any damage, but still, it's a bad precedent to set. I was going to call his dad, but didn't see the point."

"Why not?"

"His dad is a cop. Officer Buchanan," he said. "Hard to tell if he'd answer the call as dad or as the police."

# TWENTY-THREE

I hadn't wanted to see Officer Buchanan as a potential suspect in my growing list of people to watch, but the connection here was too great to ignore. Tommy himself had told me his dad dropped him off. Had Buchanan asked his son to slip the note into my towel? Or even done it himself? I already knew Buchanan knew Dr. Hall. He'd been the one to refer me to him to seek help, and he'd mentioned his own sessions with the doctor. He seemed to have taken a special interest in the case.

And of all the people who knew pieces of what I knew, Officer Buchanan was the only one who knew more. What had really been behind his sessions with Dr. Hall? Had he confided something he'd rather kept secret—something big enough to give him motive for murder? I already knew enough to know Dr. Hall wasn't honest. I just didn't know which of his activities—adultery, prescription-drug tampering, or possibly even blackmail—had been the one to get him killed.

I thanked the office manager and unlocked Emma's car. Rocky hopped into the driver's side and walked across to the passenger seat. I slid in behind him, closed the doors, and immediately locked them. Emma's mint-green convertible was about twice the size of my Alfa Romeo and it took me a few miles to get used to the large hood and extended width of the car. We were in the middle of the desert, a picturesque utopia of palm trees, greenery, and flat-roofed houses, yet the peaceful environment felt off, like I was looking at it through glasses with a shattered lens. I followed the directions to the strip mall and parked. My first phone call was to Hudson.

"Hey, Lady," he answered. His voice sounded low and gravelly, as if he'd just woken up.

"Hey yourself. How are you feeling?"

"Like I was in a fight that the other guy won."

"Are you going to tell me what happened out there?"

"It's over. I don't want you to worry." He was quiet for a few seconds. "Omar claims they're letting me go this afternoon. You think you have what it takes to look after me while I recover?"

"Sure. I'll be in charge of sponges and swabs."

"What?"

"Doris Day joke. I might even make you watch the episode so you get it. Yes, I have what it takes. I'll let Emma know."

"Has she heard anything about Jimmy?"

"Not as far as I know." I didn't want to stress Hudson out by pressing him for answers, not yet. "Emma and Heather stayed with me at the Tiki motel last night."

"Why didn't you stay at the house with them?"

"Long story. We'll talk about it when I see you."

"Hey, Madison?"

"Yes?"

"I know this trip was about seeing my sister and working for my brother-in-law, but the longer I lay in this hospital bed, the more the only thing I'm thinking about is spending the night alone with you."

"You and me both."

I hung up and sat in the parking lot. Rocky walked across the front seat and stuck his head out of my window. "What do you think, Rocky? Bagels or donuts?"

The difficult decision was postponed when my phone rang. The number was a 214 area code, which meant it was in Dallas. Possibly a client.

I answered, "Mad for Mod, Madison speaking."

"You answer the phone like that even when you're on vacation?" Tex said.

"Lieutenant, I mean, Captain Allen. This isn't your number."

"Night, I'm flattered you know my number. You're right. I'm calling from Dr. Randall's office."

Immediately my hackles rose. "Any business I have with Dr. Randall is between him and me. That means it's confidential. You have no right to nose around in my private matters."

"Whoa, Night, slow down. I'm not here because of you, I'm here because of me. But you do make me wonder if you talk about me during your sessions."

"There haven't been any sessions," I blurted.

"Yet," he said. A beat of silence passed where Tex probably gloated, and I questioned how he managed to get a rise out of me, even with a distance of thirteen hundred miles between us. "That's not why I called. I talked to your boyfriend last night. He called me from the hospital."

"Why would he call you? You're not friends."

"We have certain things in common. He told me your getaway to Palm Springs has been a little off and he asked me to check in on you."

"I don't believe for a second Hudson asked you to check on me."

"Ask him." The thought of asking Hudson was too embarrassing to entertain and Tex probably anticipated that. "So, you okay, Night? You were supposed to call me back."

"Yeah?" I said with more than a little annoyance in my voice. "Well, I've been busy."

"What's going on there? Talk to me."

Why not? Tex was the one person I could confide in, if only because of the distance between where we were. So I did. "When we talked yesterday, I told you about the victim in the river and the relationship between him and Hudson's sister."

"Yeah. You didn't tell James about his sister's affair yet, did you?"

"It's not my info to tell."

"He's in the hospital. It might be related."

"What makes you say that?"

"What makes you think it's not?"

"Seriously, Lieutenant—Captain, how did you reach that conclusion?"

"It's called routine police work."

"No, it's not. Not with three states between us, it's not, not after you took a promotion that put you behind a desk."

He sighed. "Fine. I followed up with the precinct that called me about you. Wanted to make sure you were staying out of trouble. Go ahead, let me have it. Violation of your privacy, move on, whatever you need to say. I probably crossed the line, but considering there was a murder victim, I was worried."

"Who did you talk to?"

"What?"

"Who did you talk to in Palm Springs?"

"Officer Buchanan," he said.

"Crap."

"Not the response I expected."

"Look. I have to talk to somebody and you've proven to be a good sounding board in the past. Are you willing to listen and help me out without judging me?"

"Shoot. I'll see what I can do."

"Get a pen and a piece of paper. I'm going to give you the cast of characters."

Rustling of papers replaced conversation for a few seconds. "Okay, go."

I ran my hand over Rocky's fur and stared out the front windshield. "I told you about the body, I told you about Emma and the doctor having an affair. Did I tell you Emma and Jimmy's neighbor is the doctor's ex-wife?"

He whistled. "There's a complication."

"Tell me about it. Her name is Jo Conway, and I'm not clear on how much, if anything, she knows about the affair between Emma and her ex. I'm also not clear if Emma cared if she did find out. From what Jo told me, the doctor had more than one affair."

"Sounds like a real catch."

"According to the ex-wife, she didn't have a hard time deciding on a divorce. She said he was having an affair with his receptionist and more than one of his patients when they split up. Last night, Emma told me all about how she met Dr. Hall at the local flea market. I originally thought he was her doctor, but it turns out she was never his patient. When he told her he was a doctor, he said he could get her whatever prescriptions she needed."

"Ethical too."

"Hold that thought. Next, there's the guys who beat up Jimmy and Hudson in Salton. The hospital staff referred to them as 'Benji Nalder's gang.' Officer Buchanan says Benji has a record a mile long and doesn't come to Palm Springs because he's probably wanted for something."

"What did James say about the fight? Who started it?"

I hesitated for a second. "He didn't tell me anything about it. He said he didn't want me to worry."

"How's that working out?"

"There's something else you should know about Benji. I was working by myself by a local quarry Jimmy is using as a staging area for the items he's acquired in Salton. It's part of the job I'm here to do. Some guys came up to me while I was working. I know now the main guy was Benji."

"You didn't mention this yesterday."

"I didn't think it was related."

"What did this Benji want?"

I flushed with embarrassment. "I don't know. To intimidate me? Maybe he was just being friendly." I didn't believe my own words for a second.

"You don't think he was just being friendly, do you?"

"No."

"Tell me what happened and give me all of the details. Let me decide what's pertinent and what's not."

"This group of guys walked up to me. The main one—Benji—kept calling me 'pretty lady.' He told the other guys to get lost for a few minutes, that there would be…"

"There would be what, Night?"

Even the thought of Benji's words brought back the fear. "He said there would be 'enough for everybody.'"

"What did you do?"

"I slammed my arm into the bottom of his chin and then kicked him in the crotch and ran."

"Where'd you learn self-defense?"

"I didn't. I was scared. For all I know, he's going to file assault charges. Probably if I'd told him to back off, he would have and it would have been over."

There was a pause on the other end of the phone, where I pictured Tex running his hand through his hair, staring up at the ceiling formulating a plan. Only, this wasn't Tex's precinct. He wasn't here. There wasn't anything he could do. I thought there would be value in talking things through. And in one way, there was. I felt better having acknowledged what had happened. But in terms of what I knew, I was as lost as I'd been when I woke up.

"Night, you did the right thing. Fear is an indicator something isn't right and it sounds to me like the situation could have gone a totally different direction if you'd just stood there and let it. Maybe that's what started the fight. Could be James was defending your honor."

I felt myself tense up as he talked, the rage building inside of me again. I didn't want to let it take over who I was. "I don't want to talk about that anymore."

Tex surprised me by not lecturing me on the importance of dealing with my demons. "Anything else you need to tell me about this case?"

"Somebody sent Emma's daughter to the park. They pretended to be Emma, but Emma was in the hospital with Jimmy. The park ranger called to find out if Emma was on her way."

"How old is the daughter?"

"Nine."

"Shit."

"I know. Officer Buchanan was on his way to the house with

Rocky, so he went with Emma to get Heather and talk to the park ranger."

"Okay, I got your cast of characters. Tell me what you're thinking."

"Wait. There's somebody else." I hesitated. "Officer Buchanan."

"I thought you just said he helped out with the little girl. What about him?"

"I don't know if I can trust him."

"Night, ninety-nine percent of cops aren't crooked."

"I know. And this has nothing to do with what happened in Lakewood. But Buchanan is the officer who didn't believe me when I said I found a body in the river. When I went to the police station to give them more information, he's the one who recommended I talk to Dr. Hall myself. He's a patrol officer, but he's keeping himself involved in the investigation. He's been around a lot—both officially and unofficially."

"Slow down, Night! Damn, woman. This is more mixed up than one of your Doris Day/Rock Hudson movies."

"I can't slow down. This morning, while I was swimming laps at the motel pool, somebody slipped a note between the folds of my towel. A warning. It could have been Emma, Jo, Jimmy—or Buchanan. His son is the lifeguard."

"What did it say?"

"It said it was best I start forgetting everything I knew."

"Where's this note now?"

"In the bottom of my handbag."

"I don't like coincidences."

"Neither do I."

After a short pause, Tex spoke. "I want you to go about your life the way you intended. Be a good girlfriend. Spend time with Hudson. Go shopping with his sister, take Rocky to the dog park, enjoy whatever you can about your vacation. In public. Around people. Don't go wandering off by yourself anymore. I don't care if you spot the holy grail of globe lamps tagged for five cents at a yard sale. If there's not a crowd of at least five people, you leave it alone. Be a normal person—at least as normal as you can be in those clothes you wear."

I ignored his dig at my wardrobe. "You want me to just pretend nothing happened?"

"I want you to let the police do their job."

"But the police—Buchanan—might be in on it."

"You leave Buchanan to me."

# TWENTY-FOUR

*Tex*

The conversation ended the way every conversation between Tex and Madison did: him telling her what to do and her getting angry. When was she going to realize it wasn't a feminist thing? He was a cop. She was a decorator. If one of them was equipped to handle a potentially crooked police officer, it was the one with the badge. The last time he checked, the only thing she pinned to the left breast side of her outfit was a vintage metal pin shaped like a daisy.

Tex glanced down at the notepad on the desk. It was a habit of his to scribble notes, bullet points, leads, or questions related to whatever information came in. He hadn't expected Madison to open up and tell him what was going on, but when she did, his habits had taken over. The notepad, like the office and the phone, belonged to the department shrink. Tex knew exactly what he'd been doing when he'd taken advantage of the unfamiliar phone number to check in on Madison. After Hudson James had called him from the hospital, he'd found himself in an awkward position. The two men were far from friends, but they'd been thrown together too many times to pretend neither one existed. Truth was, he thought the idea of tricking Madison with an unfamiliar phone number was funny, at least until he heard details of what was going down in California.

The door to the office opened and Peter walked in. "I see we're going for a role reversal today. Do you want to be the doctor and I'll be the patient? I'd be more than happy to play you for a session.

Maybe if you heard your issues coming from my mouth, you'd be more willing to talk about them."

Tex tapped the end of his pen against the notepad in front of him. "My issue is Madison Night. She's mixed up in some trouble in Palm Springs and there's nothing I can do about it."

Peter leaned back and tented his fingers. "Palm Springs has a police department and I'm sure they're as capable of helping her as you are. Is that really what's bothering you?"

After a few seconds, Tex threw the pen onto the desk and looked up at the doc. "No, it's not. You want to know the truth? I think I'm in love with her, but she's with somebody else. How long is it going to take to tackle that one?"

# TWENTY-FIVE

I went with the bagels. Loaded down with a dozen assorted, a gallon of cream cheese, and two large iced coffees, I returned to the car. I nestled the coffees in the cup holder and set the food on the passenger-side seat.

Before leaving the lot, I called the hospital. I was transferred three times before finally getting a chance to correct "James Hudson" to "Hudson James." The curses of having two first names. Again, I was given only the most perfunctory of information: he'd been a patient, he'd been moved, he'd been released. Aside from the inconvenience of it all, I was mildly impressed with their dedication to maintaining patient confidentiality. By the time we cleared up the confusion, I was told he had checked himself out.

I called his cell. "Hey, Lady," he said.

"I heard you were given a clean bill of health."

"Not quite clean, but not serious enough to tie up a bed for another night. Where are you at?"

"Parking lot. I went out for breakfast. Emma and Heather are sleeping in."

"Exactly how big is this room?"

"Let's put it this way. Three girls and two animals was a little tight."

"I talked to Jimmy after I was released. He said he's expecting to leave later today. I'm pretty sure that motel room is going to be a whole lot more empty tonight."

"Not too empty, I hope."

"I'd say it's going to feel just about right."

"Do you want to meet us there now? I have enough bagels for one more," I said.

"Jimmy asked me to follow up on a couple of building permits for him. Not sure how long my energy level's going to hang in there, but between him and me, he's the one who should be lying in a bed. Probably going to keep me busy for the better part of the day. How about I meet you there tonight? Around five?"

If I didn't know any better, I'd think Hudson was avoiding me. But we were there to do a job, and he was right: collapsed lung and broken ribs trumped mild concussion—only barely. I made him promise to meet me earlier than he'd said, my way of making sure he didn't overdo things.

I headed back to the motel. Emma and Heather were both up, showered, and dressed. Heather sat on the bed, running her hand over Mortiboy's head and back. Mortiboy looked a notch above tolerant.

As soon as Rocky entered the room, all hell broke loose. Mortiboy jumped down from the bed and tried to scramble underneath it. The bed was on a platform, so Mortiboy's escape route was thwarted. Rocky, delighted his friend had chosen to play, yipped and bounced around him while he dropped his head low to the ground and looked for someplace else to hide. It was like watching the pet version of the Super Bowl with a particularly pesky defensive end holding the line. Mortiboy hissed at Rocky, who backed away, giving Mortiboy a clear path to the bathroom. Heather clapped like it had been a performance orchestrated all for her.

"Have you heard from Jimmy?" I asked Emma.

"They're completing his paperwork right now. I didn't know you'd be gone so long. I want to pick him up at the hospital."

"I'm sorry," I said, holding the keys out toward her. "I had a hard time deciding between bagels and donuts."

"There's donuts?" Heather asked. "I can eat ten donuts if I'm hungry."

Emma and I exchanged a look. "I got bagels."

"Oh," the little girl said. "I can only eat two of them." I held out the bag and she rooted through it, looking for one of her choosing.

Emma put her hand on top of the bag. "There's no time for that. We're going to go pick up Daddy."

"I'm sure Jimmy is just as hungry as Heather. Let me have one and you take the rest with you."

"Aren't you coming with us?"

I shook my head. "Leave me your bike. You three deserve your own time. I'm going to pretend this really is a vacation for Hudson and me. Call me later. Maybe we can go shopping tomorrow." I pulled out a rye bagel, tore it open, and added a blob of cream cheese. I set the whole thing on a napkin and handed the bag to Emma.


There was something comforting about being alone in the motel room in the middle of the day, and it wasn't just the air conditioning. Once Emma and Heather had left, the animals settled in on separate beds, and I set up shop on the small desk in the corner. I opened the thick curtains all the way but left the glass doors shut to block out the heat. A couple of years running a business in Dallas and I could have written a book: *How To Enjoy The Summer Even When The Temps Are Over 100*. It would probably need a better title.

Tex had told me to go about life as usual. I suspected it wasn't just him telling me to mind my own business. If I did the things I'd normally do, I wouldn't look suspicious. If someone was keeping an eye on me, they'd think I took their advice. Anybody not in the business of decorating would quickly tire of outdoor flea markets and estate sales.

I cleaned Mortiboy's makeshift litter box and put out a bowl of fresh water. He seemed slightly more accepting of me than he had in the past, and I wondered if the compare/contrast of me vs. Heather from a cat's perspective had somehow boosted my stock in trade.

\*    \*    \*

Five hours, three yard sales, and a half of a canister of sunscreen later, I rode Emma's bike back to the motel. I passed up three hand-carved Tikis, a Taylorware "Cathay" casserole dish, and a large Witco wall hanging both gorgeous and too cumbersome to carry.

I locked Emma's bike in the rack inside the motel gates and lowered Rocky to the ground. He stretched the length of his leash and peed on a shrub. We scaled the stairs to the second floor while I rooted around in my small handbag for the motel room key. When I opened the door, I gasped.

The floor and the bed were littered with pink rose petals. Hudson stood next to the balcony, dressed in a black suit, white shirt, and skinny tie. His hair was parted on the side and slicked back, and his sideburns had been trimmed. While it was safe to assume he'd gone scruffy in the hospital, tonight he was clean shaven.

I closed the door behind me and dropped Rocky's leash. Rocky ran forward and hopped up on his hind legs, front paws on Hudson's knees. Hudson never took his eyes off me. "Hey, Lady," he said quietly.

"Hey, yourself," I said back. I glanced down at my pink and white gingham outfit. "Suddenly I feel wildly underdressed."

He reached behind him and pulled a bottle of champagne out of a silver ice bucket. "I had a feeling you'd feel that way," he said. "I left your outfit in the bathroom." At my shocked expression, he added, "It's the only other room here."

I took a step toward him and he pointed the opposite direction. "I'll still be here when you get back," he said.

In the bathroom was a white dress with tiny lilac flowers embroidered on it. The neckline was cut straight across but had thick straps on either side, and a lilac grosgrain ribbon was draped through loops on either side of the waist. I slipped off my top and trousers and stepped into the dress and zipped up the back. I tied the ribbon into a bow behind me and whirled around to see my reflection.

Even with liberal sunscreen applications, I'd gotten some sun. Freckles had appeared across my nose, and I dusted loose powder over them. I touched up my mascara, perked up my hair with my fingers, and then went back out front. "Where—how—" I stammered.

"There's a thrift store attached to the hospital. Lots of the rich ladies of Palm Springs donate their clothes to raise money. That dress had Madison Night written all over it."

"And your suit?"

He slid his thumbs under the narrow lapels and tipped his head down, and then raised his deep brown eyes and smiled at me. "I might have picked this up in Dallas," he said. "For a special occasion." He handed me a flute of champagne.

Music from the pool floated up to our room. It was a pop ballad, not a big band classic like I would have selected or the Ramones like Hudson would have played in his garage workshop, but it was perfect. After everything that had happened since we arrived, I'd never have predicted that a night like this was in my future. I reached my hand up and ran my fingertips over the cut by his eyebrow.

"Seems like a special occasion to me." I clinked his glass with mine and took a sip. He slid an arm around my waist and I felt his face next to my hair.

"Does this hurt?" I asked softly, concerned about his recent hospital stay.

"Not with you."

I closed my eyes and rested my head gently against his shoulder. If ever there was a time to open up to Hudson, this was it. But Hudson's injuries and weakened state dictated otherwise. Our first romantic night in the motel room ended with painkillers (his), sleeping pills (mine), and a half-full bottle of bubbly growing warm in the champagne bucket on the balcony.

\*    \*    \*

The next morning, I woke to sunlight streaming into the room. Hudson turned to me. "Morning swim?" he asked.

"Not today." I didn't want to worry him by acknowledging the note in the towel, but I also didn't want to encourage a repeat correspondence. "How about we spend the day doing Palm Springs stuff? I know Rocky's expecting a rain check on Elvis's house. We can get the map at the visitor's center and make a day of seeking out houses of the rich and famous."

"In other words, be tourists?"

"Yes. Let's be tourists."

Hudson laughed. "Sounds like a plan."

I pulled a green and white striped top and a white skort trimmed in green (Simplicity #7499) from my bag, along with a fresh set of underwear, and headed to the shower. My look was low-maintenance on the best of days, and the Palm Springs temperature made it even lower. I was ready for a day of leisurely tourist activities fifteen minutes after we'd made the plan. Unfortunately, even the best laid plans are often overturned.

When I opened the bathroom door, I heard the TV. A reporter's voice confirmed the fact I'd suspected for days. "The body pulled out of Whitewater River earlier this week has been identified as that of local resident, Dr. Albert Hall. High levels of painkillers in his system originally indicated suicide, but based on evidence found at the scene, the police are not ruling out foul play."

I watched the screen from outside the bathroom. The reporter went on to say the police had several suspects and they were trying to establish a timeline for the murder. I stepped out from where I'd been standing and looked at Hudson. "I have to call them," I said.

"You've already done enough. You told them everything you know."

"No, Hudson, I haven't. The SUV that almost ran us off the road the day we arrived? It was him."

"It was who?"

"Dr. Albert Hall. Him." I pointed at the screen. "The body I saw in the river."

"How do you know?"

I closed my eyes, silently begged Emma to forgive me, and then opened my eyes. "Your sister told me. She asked me not to tell you, but I think things have gotten out of control."

"I don't get it. What does Emma have to do with any of this? What did she ask you not to tell?"

"She and the doctor were having an affair and now she thinks his death is her fault."

# TWENTY-SIX

"Where'd you hear that?" Hudson asked.

"I told you, she confided in me."

He stood up and pulled a clean black T-shirt from his luggage. "I don't believe it." He winced as he pulled the shirt over his bandaged ribs.

"You think I'm lying?" I asked.

"No—not you. I don't believe she'd be dumb enough to do something like this." He shook his head from side to side.

I rushed forward and put my hands on his forearms. "She and Jimmy have been having trouble. When she came to visit you in Dallas, it was supposed to be a trial separation."

"She told you that too?"

I nodded. "She didn't want you to know because she didn't know if they'd get back together or not. She was afraid you'd treat him differently. She knows you two are friends."

"But she's my sister. If I'm going to take a side, it's going to be hers."

"Are you?"

"What?"

"Going to take a side?"

"She went back to him. There's no side to take."

"Hudson, she had an affair. The man is dead. Maybe she's been able to keep it a secret up to now, but there's a good chance as the police dig into Dr. Hall's background, they're going to discover her connection to him. I don't know if Jimmy knows or not, but no matter which way this goes, she's going to need your support."

We stood like that for a couple of seconds, my hands on Hudson's forearms, him staring at me, searching my face for answers I couldn't provide.

"Do you know anything else about Dr. Hall?" he asked.

I moved my hands down his arms and laced my fingers through his. I looked down at the carpet and turned away from Hudson and led him to the unmade bed. After I sat down, I gently tugged on his hand. He sat next to me. I looked back at his face.

"Boy, do I ever."

It took over an hour to catch Hudson up on the romantic life and times of Dr. Albert Hall. Having run through the facts one time already with Tex, I was less jumbled this time.

"I think the men who attacked you and Jimmy in Salton were the same ones who approached me at the quarry."

"What makes you say that?"

"Something Omar told me. He's the orderly who took care of my tetanus shot. I ran into him in the ER the day you went to the hospital and he told me what he overheard you tell the police."

Hudson nodded and looked down at his hands. "When Jimmy and I were first going over this job, he told me where we'd be working in Salton. Your sketchpad was nearby and I wrote the details down in it. Where we'd be working, where the quarry was, who was on the team."

"So Benji knew about the job site in Salton from me—because I left my sketchpad behind. If I hadn't left it, you wouldn't have gotten hurt."

"Madison, those guys jumped us because they wanted something and we didn't have it. I don't know what it was, but the fight wasn't a random attack. The only reason we're in such bad shape is because it was four against two."

"Did you report it?"

He looked at me. "No."

"Why not?"

"Because I'm the one who threw the first punch." He took a breath and coughed a couple of times. I put my hand on his chest, as if I could somehow take the pain away with my touch. "I have no doubts there would have been a fight, but I'm the one who started it. Benji asked us if we brought it, if we were his new contact. Jimmy played it cool, said we didn't want any trouble. We were about to leave when Benji said something about you."

"Me?"

"He said to tell the pretty lady at the quarry next time he wouldn't be so nice." He moved my hand from his chest. "Even if I hadn't seen one of your sketches sticking out of his back pocket, I would have known he meant you. I slugged him. Jimmy jumped in. You know the rest."

We finished sharing what we knew. I expected him to say exactly what Tex had said, but Hudson was more concerned with Emma and her involvement in Dr. Hall's life. He recognized I could take care of myself, but there was a chance his sister wasn't as strong as I was. If anybody needed his protection, it was her.

As I spoke, Hudson drew a stick figure on a blank postcard left in the room and labeled it "Dr. Hall." He connected lines around it like a George Nelson ball clock, and wrote in every person who had a connection to him. On a separate page, he made a list of suspects: Jo Conway, Benji Nalder, Officer Buchanan, Jimmy McKenna. He labeled each one—ex-wife, thug, cop, as if making a cast of characters for a program in the theater district. He left the space after Jimmy's name blank.

"You have to write Emma's name on there too," I said gently. Before he got the wrong idea, I put my hand on his. "I'm not saying she's responsible, but she is involved. Somehow. If we ignore that, we put her at risk."

He wrote her name down on the side of the paper, but used a dotted line to connect her back to Dr. Hall. "What do we do now?" he asked.

"Nothing. There's nothing we can do."

The look on Hudson's face was sweet and helpless at the same time. Despite the lifetime of curveballs and tragedies that had aged him, right now, he looked like a kid. "She's my sister," he said. "She's the only family I have. She's going to get hurt. I can't do nothing."

I stood up. "Then we go back to the river where I first saw the body. Where it all started."

"No," he said. He shook his head, and for a split second I thought he was having second thoughts about getting involved. "If everything you've said is true, it started the day we arrived in Palm Springs, when Dr. Hall almost drove us off the road."


I took Rocky out for a brisk walk while Hudson attended to Mortiboy's litter box. We left the animals with fresh water, food, and the TV turned to the nature channel. Hudson drove to the street where Emma and Jimmy lived and parked at the entrance. A hand-painted sign cautioning drivers to slow down had been nailed onto a tree. Jimmy must have added it after our accident like he said he would.

I stepped out of the car and misted myself with sunscreen and then turned the nozzle toward Hudson. He put one hand on the hood of the Jeep for balance and braced himself as if I were about to spray him with pepper spray instead of Coppertone Sport 50+. I blasted his face and then each of his arms. His legs, clad in his standard faded blue jeans, were safe from whatever the sun cast his way.

We walked slowly down the road toward the scene of the accident. I could tell Hudson was still hurt, though he pretended otherwise. He had called Emma before we headed out of the motel and mentioned we were taking the day to play tourist. He casually mentioned we might stop by, but nothing definite. I'd offered him privacy while he made the call, but he told me to stay. Regardless of what he thought of his sister's actions, he kept any judgment out of his voice. Now that we were here, wandering around their neighborhood, I think both of us hoped we'd fly under their radar.

"What are we looking for?" I asked.

"I don't know. It's been almost a week since the accident."

We split up, Hudson following the tree line to the hairpin turn where he'd been trapped inside the car, and me shuffling along the opposite direction, scanning the ground from left to right with every step I took. The dry dirt left a coating over my sneakers, and I was happy I'd had the foresight not to wear sandals. No matter how gently I stepped, I ended up with a trace of dirt around the topline of the shoes, which turned into grit inside. Both my sneakers and my feet were going to be in need of a scrubbing by the time this adventure was over.

I pulled my sunscreen out of my bag and sprayed my bare legs with a second coating. The spray left a shiny residue behind. I turned around to see if Hudson was anywhere close, and when he wasn't, I pulled my halter away from my chest and sprayed there too. Sunburned cleavage wasn't attractive on anybody.

I wedged the can of sunscreen under one arm, put my hand under the neckline of my striped top, and rubbed the sunscreen in so as to make it appear less like a coating of shellac. When I finished, the palms of my hands were greasy. I tried to move the sunscreen and it slipped from between my fingers and landed on the ground. With no other options, I wiped my hands on my skort, shaking my head at the dirty handprints I left behind, and then looked on the ground for the can. It had rolled a few feet away and came to rest against what appeared to be a rock.

Only it wasn't. The closer I got, the more I knew the rock wasn't a geological formation; it was a crushed amber pill vial ground into the loose gravel at the edge of someone's driveway.

And all of a sudden, I didn't care so much about getting dirty.

# TWENTY-SEVEN

I dropped down to my hands and knees and used my fingers to claw dirt away from the broken amber vial. The portion of the label that was showing was mostly faded thanks to exposure to the desert sun. It took a while to get enough of the dirt dug out from underneath the bottle for me to get a grip on it without breaking it further. I slowly tugged on the edge of the vial and wiggled it back and forth against the ground until it came loose. A shadow cast across the portion of the ground where I was stooped.

"So you're the one who's been snooping around my property. Can I help you?" asked a man's voice. I looked up and saw an older man, somewhere in his eighties or nineties, standing in front of me. He was dressed in a short-sleeved Hawaiian print shirt unbuttoned over a thin undershirt, madras plaid shorts, white socks, and the kind of rubber sandals I'd seen people wear around the pool to keep from getting foot fungus.

The strain on my knees was too great for me to remain where I was, so reluctantly, I pushed myself up to a standing position. A zing of pain shot through my bad knee and I bucked back down to the ground. "Ow!" I uttered.

"Madison?" Hudson shouted.

Slowly, I stood up again. I shifted my stance so my sneaker rested on top of the vial, obstructing it from view. I turned to the man. "I'm sorry. Bad knee."

"You don't get to be my age without knowing the pain of bad joints," the man said. "Ernie Middleton," he said. He held out his hand.

"Madison Night." Hudson rounded the corner. He had one arm wrapped around his ribs. When he saw Ernie, he dropped his arm. "This is Hudson James," I added.

Ernie let go of my hand and shook Hudson's. "I saw you looking around. Lose something?"

Hudson spoke first. "We took a pretty hard turn out here a few days ago and our Jeep tipped over."

I smiled a somewhat sheepish smile and jumped in. "I didn't realize it at the time, but I think my overnight kit opened up and spilled out a few items. I convinced Hudson to bring me back and help me look."

"My wife told me about that. Said she saw a car tipped over. Never saw a car tip over before. When I looked out the window, there was no car. I told her she imagined it." He looked at Hudson. "Is that how you hurt your head?"

Hudson nodded slowly. "Freak thing. My friend came along and helped flip the car back over before things got worse. No damage to the car, so we drove off."

Ernie turned back to me. "I think I might be able to help you out with what you lost from your overnight kit," he said. "You want to follow me inside?"

I misunderstood his offer.

"It's not important. I can replace just about all of it with a trip to the drug store."

"Won't take but a minute. 'Course if you want to wait here in the hot sun, it's your choice."

I glanced at Hudson. He looked as surprised by Ernie's generosity as I was. Before either of us had a chance to respond, he turned around and headed toward his carport.

"What is he planning on giving you?" Hudson asked in a low voice.

"I have no idea. I said overnight kit because I thought it was generic enough it would sound believable, but personal enough that there wouldn't be any questions."

"Quick thinking," he said. "But I gotta say, I'm curious. For all we know, you're about to become the beneficiary of a very large jug of Metamucil."

I punched him lightly on the upper arm. "Be nice," I said. "That could be you one day."

He shook his head. "He lost me with the white socks. Mine are going to be black."

"I'll remember that." I reached around the back of my head and pulled my hair off the nape of my neck to try to cool down. When I looked back at the carport, the door was open, but Ernie wasn't there.

The carport, a popular feature on houses from the mid-fifties, was attached to a gem of a structure. It was a white ranch with a butterfly roof. The front yard was a perfect example of Xeroscaping, where grass had been replaced with a yard of pebbles and rocks set about in a pleasing display. Pinkish pavers were nestled throughout, creating a path that led to the front door. A bright bougainvillea, popular in this dry climate thanks to its minimal water consumption, sat by the front porch, the only jolt of color against the otherwise muted residence.

As I stared at the house, admiring the details, the front door opened and a woman stared out at us. She held a serving tray with a pitcher of lemonade and four glasses. "Well, don't just stand there," she said to us. "I'm letting all the air out of the house. Come on, lemonade is getting warm." She turned around and the door slowly swung shut behind her.

Ernie came out of a door on the side of the carport with an olive canvas duffel bag in his grip. "She means business. You want your bag, you're going to have to drink lemonade with Eunice." He shuffled to the front steps and went inside. The door slapped shut behind him too, but he turned back and spoke to us through the screen. "Come on, you heard her," he said.

Hudson leaned down behind me and spoke in my ear. "Do you recognize that bag?" he asked quietly.

"I think so."

"Is it yours?"

"Nope." I turned my head and looked up at Hudson. "Ernie thinks it fell out of the Jeep when we tipped."

"But it didn't."

"The last time I saw a bag like that was on the pier the morning I saw the body in the water. Emma said she saw Albert throw a bag like that onto the passenger side seat of the truck. Are you as curious as I am?"

He smiled. "Let's go have some lemonade."


Eunice and Ernie Middleton lived in the kind of house I dreamed about. The interior was what mid-century enthusiasts called a time capsule: decorated and maintained in the original style from the middle of the previous century. The foyer and living room were carpeted with bright green wall-to-wall carpeting. The sofa and chairs were upholstered in a cheery green, yellow, and white stripe, and an accent chair coordinated with a whimsical daisy print fabric. A bowl of potpourri sat on a boomerang coffee table, and a small metal stand bursting with magazines was tucked between the daisy chair and a green floor lamp. Behind the sofa hung a pair of large Maio paintings featuring young women dressed in harlequin costumes. The girl in the painting on the left wore a yellow and white costume and held a black cat; on the right, the subject wore shades of green and held a violin.

This was exactly the type of estate I tried to discover by reading the obituaries every morning. In the first thirty seconds I spotted several pieces I'd love to add to my inventory. In the immediate couple of seconds after, I cringed at the morbid connection between those two thoughts.

"You have a lovely home," I said to Eunice.

"Most people think it's old fashioned," Ernie said. Ernie had settled down into the sofa. He held half of a windmill cookie. The other half appeared to be sprinkled in the form of crumbs down the front of his shirt.

"Not Madison," Hudson said. "She's a decorator."

Eunice cast me a sideways glance. "You probably want me to throw it all out and paint the place beige."

"No!" I said quickly. "Absolutely not. It's perfect the way it is."

"Do you hear that, Ernie? Perfect. From a decorator." She looked at me and smiled. "It was featured in one of those magazines," she said. "Want to see?"

To anybody else, sitting in that living room three feet from the olive duffel bag that possibly held a clue to the murder of Dr. Hall, agreeing to see the magazine where Ernie and Eunice Middleton's house had been profiled might have been torture. To me, it was a much-needed respite. Decorating was the one thing I did without thinking. It was what calmed me when I was stressed and was the most satisfying thing I could do with my time. That duffel bag could sit there all day for all I cared.

Or at least for the next fifteen minutes. I could ignore it for fifteen minutes, I was pretty sure.

Maybe even twenty.

Eunice pulled a magazine out of a brass rack next to her orange tweed chair. She handed Hudson the magazine. "Page twenty-three," she said.

"How long have you lived here?" I asked.

"Since 1956," she said. "The year we were married."

"'56," I repeated. "That was a good year."

"You're too young to know anything about 1956," Ernie said.

"That's the year *The Man Who Knew Too Much* came out," I said. "Doris Day was thirty-two. She was so upset by the treatment of the animals on set a lot of people think it's what led to her becoming an animal rights activist."

Ernie got a sour look on his face and flapped his hand at me in a gesture that made me stop talking. "That's a remake," he said. "The original was better. Peter Lorre, now there's an actor."

Eunice reached over and slapped Ernie's knee. "You're old, but you're not that old," she said.

"I saw it when it came out," he said proudly. He turned back to Hudson and me. "I was eight years old. My dad used to give me a nickel and drop me off in front of the theaters. In those days you could pay for a movie and stay in the theater all day watching it over and over. I saw *The Man Who Knew Too Much* three times."

I had never seen the original, but if it was anything like the Doris Day remake, where Doris Day's son is kidnapped in a foreign location, I questioned the impact the storyline would have on an impressionable eight-year-old boy.

Hudson spoke up. "Madison is something of a Doris Day expert," he said. "They share a birthday, and—and—" He looked at me. "What was your first Doris Day movie?"

"*Pillow Talk*, of course," I said, and we all laughed. "I didn't see *The Man Who Knew Too Much* until much later. Hitchcock bought back the rights to it as part of his legacy to his daughter, so it was largely unseen until the eighties."

"I didn't know that," Hudson said.

"There were others too, but I don't know which they were."

Ernie sat up a little straighter. "*Rope, Rear Window, The Trouble with Harry*, and *Vertigo*," he said. "They're called 'the Five Lost Hitchcocks.'"

"Ernie used to work at the theater downtown," Eunice said. The expression on her face changed from mild annoyance at his cookie-eating abilities to pride in his knowledge. She reached forward and brushed the crumbs off his shirt.

"Thanks, honey," he said. He took her hand and squeezed it. "Why don't you give the young lady a tour?" he asked her. "She hasn't touched her lemonade or her cookies. I think she's going to burst if you don't show her the aqua bathroom."

"You have an aqua bathroom?" I asked.

Eunice dabbed at her lipstick with a cloth napkin and then set it down on the coffee table. "Come with me, dear."

The tour lasted well over fifteen minutes. Thoughts of the olive duffel bag had all but been replaced by the interior of Eunice and Ernie's house. Not only did they have an aqua bathroom, but their bedroom had yellow and white daisy wallpaper and a green shag rug. If the house had been for sale, I would have made an offer.

When Eunice and I returned to the living room, Hudson and Ernie were sitting on the sofa watching the TV. The plate of cookies was empty. At this rate, we'd be moved in by dinner. Ernie reached for the remote and clicked off the TV, and then stood up, keeping one hand on his lower back.

He turned to Hudson. "You two seem like a nice enough couple," he started. "And I know the kids today look for something entirely different from what Eunice and I were looking for when we first started dating, but I think you two are going about this all wrong."

It should have been charming—funny even—having this lovely older couple calling Hudson and I "kids" and giving us advice on how to date, but something about the tone of his voice felt off.

Hudson didn't pick up on it. "Madison and I have known each other for a couple of years, but we only just started dating recently," he said. "I appreciate your perspective, but I think we'd like to let our relationship take its course on its own."

Ernie flapped his hand in Hudson's direction the same way he did when he'd been trying to cut me off earlier. "I'm not talking about your relationship, son. That's none of my business. I'm talking about this," he said. He picked up the olive duffle bag and shook it at Hudson. "You think I didn't look inside? You think I don't know what you're really up to?" He tossed the bag on the sofa behind him.

"Ernie!" Eunice said. "You said you'd keep quiet."

"You shush, woman. I've just been waiting for someone to show up and start asking about that bag. It's a good thing I called the cops when they got here."

"The cops? Why would you call the cops?" I asked. I looked at Ernie and then Eunice, and then back at Ernie.

"Fell out of your car, my ass." He glanced at his wife as if anticipating a second reprimand. She wrung her hands but said nothing. "You seem nice enough, but I think it's an act. I don't know what you're up to, but I do know everything you've said since I found you in my driveway is a lie."

He unzipped the duffle and dumped out several gallon-sized plastic freezer bags filled with pills.

# TWENTY-EIGHT

Eunice gasped. "Ernie! Where did you get all those pills?"

"That bag I found in the driveway," Ernie said.

"That bag doesn't belong to you. You had no business looking inside," Eunice said.

"Yeah? Well it's a good thing I did. These two here are up to something. They were out front digging around in the bushes looking for it."

I looked at Hudson. I didn't know if we were thinking the same thing. The problem was I didn't know for sure what I was thinking. Emma had told me she suspected that Dr. Hall had been up to something illegal, and Dr. Hall had practically driven us off the road at this very spot. Now it turned out a bag of pills had been found nearby.

But Emma had said she saw him throw the bag on the passenger-side seat of the truck. That meant the bag hadn't fallen out of the truck. If anything, it had been thrown. Whoever had expected Dr. Hall to show up with those had been disappointed. I had a feeling that meeting hadn't gone as planned.

We had to tell the cops. That likely meant Buchanan. What if he was involved?

The last thing Tex had said to me when we spoke was to leave Buchanan to him. But Tex was thirteen hundred miles away. His job was to protect the people of Lakewood, Texas, not me. Besides, I didn't know how to explain to Hudson that I'd called Tex for help. If Buchanan showed up at the Middletons' front door, then we were going to have to deal with that head on.

There was a knock at the door. I stiffened. I'd expected sirens to announce the approach of the police, but it seemed this wasn't that kind of call. If Buchanan had taken the call, and he was crooked, would he be able to keep the call under wraps and come here by himself?

Ernie turned to his wife. "Eunice, get the door." He bent down and shoveled the bags of pills back into the duffel bag.

"Don't touch them," I said.

"Huh?"

"I don't know where those pills came from, but the police are probably going to consider that entire bag as evidence. There might be fingerprints on it."

Ernie looked like he'd been hit with a bug zapper. He dropped one of the bags and it split open on contact with the floor, scattering oblong cornflower blue tablets under the sofa and chair. A couple rolled toward the toe of my sneaker. I bent down and picked one up. On one side, it said OC. The other had "160" printed on it.

Only a person who'd been on prescription painkillers would immediately recognize the OC as OxyContin.

It was what I'd been prescribed after the skiing accident that tore my ACL, but in a dose much lower than this. I'd written off my reaction to the drug—nausea, vomiting, and dizziness—to what was arguably a nervous breakdown brought on by emotional stress, and as soon as my body could tolerate the pain, had switched to Ibuprofen and flushed the Oxy tablets down the toilet. Since then, the news had reported on drug-related deaths linked to OxyContin. The base of the drug was an opioid, and it seemed there were people out there who crushed, snorted, and injected the pill as a way to get high. But what struck me the most about the blue pill between my fingertips was the number 160. I'd been prescribed 80mg, a dosage that had been discontinued in 2011 because of the dangerous risk of misuse. Just one of those pills had incapacitated me with side effects. What would double that amount do?

"Ms. Night, Mr. James," said Detective Drayton.

"Detective Drayton," Hudson said. "I think there's been a mix-up."

"No, wait. I don't think so." They all turned to me, and I turned to Hudson. "Until today we had no proof our accident by the hairpin turn had anything to do with Dr. Hall's death. But now we do. This duffel bag, the pills, they connect everything. We have to tell them."

"Tell us what?" Ernie asked.

"Ms. Night, are you suggesting you've been withholding evidence?" Detective Drayton asked.

"The only person here who's been withholding evidence is Ernie Middleton."

Everybody in the room turned to face the old man. He clutched the now-empty duffel bag to his chest and looked at the rest of us. Eunice stepped closer to him but slightly behind, as if they were Bonnie and Clyde and we were the FBI. Detective Drayton looked back at me. He seemed to be waiting for an explanation.

"This past Monday when Hudson and I arrived in Palm Springs, our car was almost run off the road on the way to his sister's house. The Jeep flipped over and Hudson was trapped inside it. At the time we thought it was a freak accident."

"It didn't occur to you to report the accident to the police?" Drayton asked.

"Why would we? Nobody was hurt. The other driver didn't stick around, so we had no leads on how to find him. The Jeep is part of Jimmy's fleet and any damage to it will be covered by insurance. We were eager to get to Hudson's sister's house, which was less than a mile from where the Jeep tipped over."

"Why'd you come back here today?"

I snuck a quick glance at Hudson. So far everything I'd said had been true, but I was about to veer off into grayer territory. "I think something fell out of my overnight bag when the car tipped, so we came back here to look around and see if we could find it."

The vague nature of "overnight bag" didn't have the same

effect on Detective Drayton as it had on Ernie when we'd first arrived. "What was missing?" the detective asked.

"Her dope," Ernie spoke up. He picked up a plastic bag of pills and shook them at me. "She's some kind of dealer. Look at this stuff. Palm Springs is a clean town. We don't need people like her bringing big-city crime with them."

The humor of a blonde, blue-eyed, middle-aged woman in vintage green and white golf clothes being at the head of a prescription drug scandal was lost on everybody in the room.

"Detective Drayton," I said calmly. "Ernie Middleton told us he found that duffel bag after his wife saw a car tip in front of his house last Monday. That tipped car was ours. He mistakenly thought the duffel belonged to us, but instead of either coming to our aid or contacting you to turn in the evidence, he kept the bag in his garage. Before you arrived here, he admitted to having looked at the contents. Doesn't it seem odd that someone would find a duffel bag filled with prescription drugs and not call the police?"

"Ernie, honestly. She's right. What did you think you were going to do with those pills?" Eunice asked.

"They were blue. At first I thought they were—you know—"

"Ernie!" Eunice blushed a deep shade of red. She turned around and disappeared into the kitchen.

Ernie shook his head. "I know now they're not Viagra, but I didn't then. Seemed like I was doing the world a favor by keeping them off the street."

Detective Drayton cleared his throat and appeared to fight a smile. "Mr. Middleton, why don't you go check on your wife while I talk to Ms. Night."

"Good idea." Ernie shuffled into the kitchen after Eunice.

Detective Drayton turned to Hudson. "Mr. James, I wonder if you could give Ms. Night and me a couple of minutes alone. I'd like to talk to you too when we're done."

Hudson nodded. "I'll move the car into the driveway," he said, and then left.

It had been a long day and I was tired. I sank down onto the sofa and rubbed my kneecap. The detective sat in the tweed chair across from me.

"I talked to your friend Captain Allen this morning. He says you have some concerns regarding Officer Buchanan."

It was one thing to talk over my concerns with Tex, but another to know my possibly unfounded suspicions and residual distrust of men in uniform could cost someone his career. An overwhelming sense of guilt washed over me.

"Detective, I had a confidential conversation with a friend this morning, one in which I might have led him to believe things about Officer Buchanan that were the product of my imagination. I hope your conversation with Captain Allen was about something more substantial than that."

"This investigation would be in a whole different place if Officer Buchanan had found the body the day you first saw it in the river."

"The victim was a psychiatrist named Dr. Hall, wasn't he?" I asked. Drayton nodded. "Hudson and I didn't have reason to believe he was the person driving the car that drove us off the road until recently."

"What makes you think he was?"

It wasn't the time for theorizing. I took a minute to review what I knew for sure. So many of my facts came from Emma's story. I wanted to tell the truth, but I didn't want to hurt her. "Hudson's sister lives about half a mile past the bend in the road. She said she saw the doctor get into the truck with two olive-green duffel bags." I picked up the now empty bag. "Mr. Middleton found this after the accident." I bent over and scooped up a couple of the scattered blue pills. "Do you know what these are?"

Drayton picked one of the pills up from my open palm. He held it up and looked at one side, and then looked at the back. "I have an idea. Do you?"

"I think it's OxyContin. I was prescribed 80 mg when I injured my knee. My doctor said it was the strongest thing he could give me."

"You still have a prescription?"

I shook my head. "I'm not a fan of drugs in most circumstances, and I had a bad reaction to that one. My knee still bothers me from time to time, but physical therapy has done wonders. I'll never feel like I felt before the accident, but I prefer a slight amount of pain to the side effects of the drug." I flexed my knee, stretching my leg out in front of me, and then relaxed it.

"Unfortunately, there are a lot of people out there who don't feel the same way," he said. "That's why this country has a growing drug problem."

"I'm pretty sure Dr. Hall was on the wrong side of the drug war. See the OC on the tablet?" I leaned forward and pointed to the surface of the small round pill. "A few years ago, after all the OxyContin deaths were being reported, the FDA ruled to change the formula. The new version has an 'OP' instead of an 'OC.' People used to crush the tablets, inhale them, or inject them." Involuntarily, I shuddered. Whether it was the cool air from the Middletons' AC on my formerly hot, sweaty skin, or the memory of a long needle injecting me with medication that kept me in a cloudy state while I'd recovered, I couldn't say.

"You know a lot about it."

"The stories on the news started popping up shortly after my accident. I was already on the fence about taking it, but that sealed the deal. When I went in for a checkup, my doctor told me about the change in formulation and said he'd write me a new prescription, but I turned him down. I went home and flushed my pills the same day." I looked up at Drayton. "If I'm right about these pills, they're twice the dosage of what I was given. My doctor said mine was the strongest he could prescribe. How's that possible?"

Drayton didn't answer. He glanced at the plastic bags bulging with pills stacked on the sofa. He pursed his lips and nodded his head, though I didn't think it had anything to do with what I'd said. He picked up one of the plastic bags and stared at it. "How many pills you think are in here?"

"A lot," I said. "My prescription was for a month's supply. A hundred and twenty pills, taken four times a day. My pill vial was about the size of a roll of quarters." I paused. "I don't know how many pills are in that bag, but it's a lot more than necessary for treating a torn ACL."

Drayton pulled out his phone and made a call. "Let me talk to somebody on the Narcotics Task Force," he said. "I'll hold." A few seconds later, Drayton spoke again. "I'm looking at five large bags of pills found on the side of the road. Blue. Oblong. One side says OC, the other says 160. How many?" He looked at me and held the phone away from his head. "A hundred and twenty pills takes up about the size of a roll of quarters, you said?"

"Somewhere around there," I answered.

He stared at the bag for a few seconds and then put the phone back to his ear. "I'd estimate about ten thou per bag. Uh-huh. Uh-huh. Uh-huh. You got it."

He hung up and looked at the bag for a few seconds, and then back at me. "I don't want to be presumptuous, but looks like we found ourselves a motive."

"You think Dr. Hall was part of a drug ring?"

"Looks that way. No confirmation yet, but Narcotics said the same thing you did. OxyContin 160. It was only on the market for about a year back in 2000 before it was discontinued. People have been killed for a lot less than what this is worth."

"These are fifteen-year-old pills. Would they still be any good?"

"FDA doesn't require companies to test how long their ingredients will last. Opioids don't expire."

"I'm not up on the street value of prescription drugs," I said. "How much do you think these bags are worth?"

He looked directly at me and held my stare long enough to make me uncomfortable. "According to my buddy, what we're looking at would bring in close to two million dollars."

# TWENTY-NINE

"Two million dollars for a couple of bags of pills?" I asked.

He handed me one of the full bags. "Do the math. About ten thousand pills in there, don't you think?"

I rested the bag on my thighs and used my fingers to approximate the width of the pill bottle I remembered from my own experience, and then slowly slid my fingers along the bottom of the bag and counted. "Probably around there."

"Fifty thousand pills."

"How do they sell them? By the dozen? By the bag?"

"By the pill. Forty dollars each."

"Two million dollars," I said, repeating the number his contact had given him.

He slowly nodded his head. "Depending on the exact count of these pills, it's going to be close. Biggest drug apprehension in the history of Palm Springs," he said. "Narco Squad is going to take over the investigation from here, but I'm not going to be happy until I know who killed Dr. Hall. What else can you tell me about the day your car flipped over?"

I thought back to the day we'd arrived. "I don't remember much else," I said honestly. "Truth is, it happened so fast Hudson and I don't even agree on what kind of a car caused the accident. Hudson is convinced it was a black truck."

"What do you think it was?"

"Dark blue Chevy Avalanche."

"That's pretty specific for something you don't really

remember," he said. "You think your mind is filling in holes in your memory?"

"No. I can't shake the fact that the car that ran us off the road was the same one parked at the river the day I first saw the body."

"You think the car belonged to Dr. Hall."

"I do. And I don't think it was an accident that the bag ended up here. I think he tossed the duffel out the window and planned to come back for it. Either way, if he showed up empty handed, somebody might have been angry enough to kill him." I chewed my lower lip. "Didn't you ask Officer Buchanan to get the keys from Park and Recreation?"

"Buchanan talked to one of the park rangers. She said the keys were claimed. Didn't you notice the truck wasn't there anymore?"

"I haven't been to the river in a while. I just assumed it was still there." We stared at each other for a second. If I was right about the truck at the river being the same one that drove us off the road, then it was suspicious it was suddenly gone.

"Ms. Night, we know Dr. Hall was found dead in the water, and we know the drugs in this living room have a street value high enough to be a motive for murder. What we don't know is how, if at all, those two things are connected."

"But you think they are, right?"

"It's not about what I think, it's about what I know." He stared at the bag of pills in his lap for a few seconds. "But it does seem to me Dr. Hall signed his own death certificate."


Based on what Detective Drayton had learned, conversations with Ernie and Eunice Middleton were more about fleshing out details of the pill discovery than a search for accomplices. It became pretty obvious the elderly couple had no idea of the value of the pills in the bag. Whatever Ernie thought would be his big payoff for finding the stash paled in comparison to the danger he'd put himself in by holding onto the bag in the first place.

A team from the narcotics squad came out to the house while

Drayton was finishing up with Hudson. Twice Eunice offered them coffee and cookies. The first time, they politely declined. The second time one of the team explained they weren't there for a social visit. After that, she shuffled around the kitchen, wiping the counters clean of imaginary spots and straightening the dish towels. Ernie drummed his fingers against the dining room table, adding in the occasional grunt just in case we'd forgotten he was there. It was late and I wanted to go back to the motel.

Scratch that. I didn't want to go back to the motel. My trip to the mid-century capital of the country had been a bust. Leaving Dallas had been partially about getting away from the setting of the recent string of crimes surrounding me, but at least when I was there, I had my own routine. Sleeping in my own bed, swimming at the local pool, creating proposals for new clients, and reorganizing the showroom of Mad for Mod. Even in the midst of the craziness I'd lived through, I'd been able to find my center. But here, the rug had been pulled out from under me from almost the minute we'd landed.

I wanted to go home.

Hudson and Detective Drayton joined us in the kitchen. "I think I have just about everything I need," Drayton said. He handed each of us a business card with his contact information on it. "If you think of anything else you might have forgotten to tell me today, don't hesitate to call."

Ernie took the card. "Who do I have to talk to about a reward?" he said.

"Ernie!" Eunice looked mortified.

"What? They wouldn't have a case if I hadn't taken such good care of that evidence."

Hudson cleared his throat. I bit my tongue. Detective Drayton spoke. "Mr. Middleton, somebody was murdered over this bag. By keeping it here instead of turning it over to the police, you put yourself and your wife in danger. You might still be in danger."

Ernie went pale.

Drayton stood up straight, thanked the rest of us for our time, and went out front. A few minutes later, the rest of the men followed him out the front door.

I took Hudson's hand. "Let's get out of here," I said. My normally polite manners had been shot an hour ago. I managed to say goodbye to Eunice and Ernie before beating Hudson to the car.

"I'd like to check on my sister while we're out this way," Hudson said. "Shouldn't take more than a minute or two." He stuck the key into the ignition and put the car into drive.

I put my hand on his forearm. "Hold on," I said. "How much did the detective tell you? About the pills."

"He didn't tell me anything. He asked about the accident, if I remembered anything about the car that almost hit us."

"What did you tell him?"

"That it was a black truck, just like I told you."

"Hudson, you didn't see it. Mortiboy was crying and you reached around to feed your fingers into his cage so he'd be less stressed. The car came out of nowhere."

"You still think it's the same SUV you saw parked by the river, don't you?"

"Yes."

Hudson put the car back into park. "You saw the dust cloud we kicked up the day of the accident. And today. Just walking around that driveway, we kicked up a good amount of dirt. That SUV in the lot was clean. You could see your reflection in the paint job. No way it was the same car."

"Somebody could have washed it."

"Why?"

"Because they didn't want us to recognize it. Hudson, I know we disagree on the memory here, but I know what I saw. It was the same SUV that drove us off the road. Remember how I thought it was an SUV and you thought it was a truck? It was both. Even your sister mentioned that Dr. Hall drove a truck away from her house."

"Did you tell Detective Drayton about Emma's involvement? Did she?"

"No." I put my hand on his arm. "Hudson, listen to me. We've left Rocky and Mortiboy alone in the motel room all day. Maybe Mortiboy is used to being alone all day, but Rocky isn't. I need to check on him."

Hudson's expression changed. "Take the Jeep. I can walk to Emma's. He climbed out of the car. "This is the last thing I expected when I suggested a getaway."

"Nobody expects something like this to happen," I said. "Sometimes it just does."

I drove to the motel. When I pulled into the motel carport, the manager flagged me to stop. I parked the Jeep in a space next to the carport and met the manager outside the motel lobby. "Is something wrong?" I asked.

"You bet something's wrong. First you were asking questions about Tommy and the next thing I know, I got a bunch of street thugs out here asking me about you and your friend. Said something about how they need to talk to you about the doctor who was killed. I don't want no trouble at my motel. You two need to check right now and find yourself another place to stay."

"Did you call the police?"

"Tommy's dad showed up and they took off. Scattered like cockroaches when you turn on a light."

"Did you tell Officer Buchanan about the gang? About what they said?"

"Of course I told him. I told him they were asking about you and your friend. He told me to have you give him a call when you got back."

"Listen, my friend's sister is in some trouble. I'll call the police later tonight."

"I don't think you understand. The gang wasn't interested in the guy you had here last night. They were asking about the woman with the little girl."

There was only one friend with a little girl who'd been with me at the Tiki Tropics. Emma.

"Can you describe the guys who were here?"

"I don't have to describe him. Everybody around here knows Benji."

The fight-or-flight reflex I'd had in the quarry rushed back to me. Benji knew where I was staying. There was no getting away from him.

"What did he want?"

"Don't know, don't care. I told him I don't want him or his pals hanging around. Even if they came here to buy soda from the vending machine, it's still bad for business. If word gets out he's setting up shop at my motel, I'm through."

"What did Officer Buchanan say when you told him?"

"Said to tell you to find another place to stay."

"You can't just kick us out," I said.

"Actually, I can. This isn't an apartment, it's a motel under private ownership. You've got an hour to get your stuff out of the room."

"But—"

"Sorry, ma'am. I know it's your vacation, but it's my business."

I left the office and called Hudson. "We have to leave the motel. I'll explain later," I said. "It'll take me a couple of minutes to pack up the room. I'm half tempted to get Rocky and Mortiboy and leave the rest."

"Call me when you're on your way."

As I crossed the parking lot toward our room, I noticed a dark blue Chevy Avalanche parked next to the vending machine. The driver's side window was down and the disturbing skeletal face of the man who'd taunted me at the quarry smiled out at me. I ran up the stairs to our room. I slammed the door behind me and threw all the locks.

In the room, I haphazardly tossed everything Hudson and I had unpacked back into our suitcases, not taking the time to sort through his/mine or dirty/clean. I clipped on Rocky's leash. Even Mortiboy seemed to be understand now was not the time to be difficult. As if he understood he was helping Hudson by cooperating with me, he sat in front of his carrier and let himself in when I opened the carrier gate.

I wasn't about to leave the room alone. Nervous energy kept me moving about the room, back and forth past the bed Hudson and I had shared last night. Back and forth past the trashcan, now overflowing with once-pink rose petals that had browned and shriveled up in the twenty-four hours since being part of our romantic backdrop. Back and forth past the empty wine bottle from the night Emma had spent with me in the room telling me her deepest, darkest secrets.

The day I'd checked into the motel, the manager had said he recognized my friend, he'd seen her check in with her husband. But he'd been referring to Dr. Hall, not Jimmy. Emma lived in Palm Springs with her husband. She'd have no reason to check into the motel with Jimmy—but she would with Dr. Hall. And she'd acted like she'd never been there before.

Facts were coming at me, realizations I didn't want to see. Emma had a medicine cabinet filled with prescription pills. Emma had been the one to feed me information about Dr. Hall long before anybody else knew he was the body in the river. Emma had been the one to place Dr. Hall in the Avalanche parked by the river.

Emma had provided answers to my questions almost before I'd had a chance to ask them. And Emma had asked me to keep her confidence, to not tell Hudson anything I knew.

But I had. And he was headed out to their house because he wanted to protect her. Protect her from who? Herself?

I hated every single thought that came at me, because it went against what I chose to believe. I didn't want to think Emma was a murderer.

I picked up my cell phone and called Hudson. He didn't answer. I left a message and followed it up with a text: *On my way.* Considering the accusations flooding my mind, it was the best I could do. I called the front desk. "I'm packed and ready to leave. Can someone help me get the animals and bags down from the second floor?"

"Give me a sec." He slammed down the receiver. A few seconds later, there was a knock at the door.

"Coming," I called. I grabbed the end of Rocky's leash so he wouldn't take off and I opened the door. Officer Buchanan stood on the other side.

# THIRTY

Buchanan was dressed in a plaid shirt and jeans. He held his hand out to stop me from talking. "I'm here unofficially. We need to get you out of here."

"But—"

"You're not safe here. The motel manager called me. He said Benji and his gang came by. They know you're staying here. They've probably been watching you come and go. I don't know what his beef is with you, but when Benji gets it into his head somebody owes him something, he doesn't just give up."

I backed up. "I don't owe Benji anything."

Buchanan pressed a button on his phone. A couple of seconds later, he put the phone on speaker. A voice spoke, familiar, despite the tinny tone.

"Night? Are you there? What the hell, did she hang up on me? Night!"

I grabbed the phone. "Tex?" I turned off the speaker option and held the phone to my head.

"Night. Listen to me. Buchanan is on your side. He knows he screwed up by not listening to you when you saw a body, but he's trying to make up for it by seeing this thing through. You stumbled on a doozy of a drug ring. Looks like the good doctor has been supplying discontinued drugs to some meth heads in Salton. When he stopped showing up, they came looking for him. Only a matter of time before something like this happened. You need to trust Buchanan and get out of there."

"But—"

"No but. Just go. You can trust him. He'll explain." He hung up on me.

I held the phone and stared at it. Buchanan said, "I called him for a favor. I heard about my son, about the note. You don't trust me—I get that. I know calling your captain friend was unorthodox, but everything about this case has been unorthodox. For your safety, I need you to get out of this motel room and away from here. You trust Captain Allen, so I thought it was the most effective way to cut through your doubts about me."

I looked at the officer in front of me and saw things through his eyes. He'd been accused, investigated, and ignored, but he'd gone out of his way to find a way to get me to hear what I needed to hear. I was in danger and the danger wasn't coming from him. I held the phone out. "I'm sorry."

"Make it up to me by listening to me now."

I looped Rocky's leash over my wrist and picked up Mortiboy's carrier. Buchanan grabbed the suitcases. We left the motel room and descended the stairs as quickly as possible. The Avalanche was gone from the parking lot. Two yips and one long meow were the only complaints we heard. Buchanan put my suitcase into the back of the Jeep.

"Where are you headed?" he asked.

"Hudson is at Emma and Jimmy McKenna's house. We should go there."

"I'll lead the way. Stay close."

We made quick time. Buchanan pulled past the driveway and I pulled in. He got out of his sedan and met me on the sidewalk. "Are you coming in?"

"Afraid I can't. This is an open investigation. I'm off duty, here unofficially. I'll be in the area, so if anything happens and you need me, it won't take me long to arrive, but I'm not going to jeopardize this case by letting my ego get in the way."

"Thank you," I said.

"Ms. Night, you're a brave woman," he said. "Not a lot of people I know would go out on a limb when nobody believes them.

Would have made your whole vacation a lot smoother if you'd ignored what you saw."

"That's not who I am," I said.

"So I heard. You ever think of changing professions?"

"Into what?"

"Police work."

I had a flash of Tex telling me to stay out of his investigations on more than one occasion and smiled at the idea of telling him what Buchanan suggested. "I like what I do," I said. "Besides, I'm not sure I'm cut out to wear a uniform."

He laughed. "I'm not sure anybody would want you to."

I didn't tell Buchanan I was nervous about going inside. Everything pointed to Emma lying, but I didn't know if Hudson could see it with the same clarity I could. Hudson was wearing blinders. The same kind of blinders I'd once worn when trying to prove his innocence.

I pulled the animal carriers and the luggage out of the car. The front door opened and Hudson joined me. He grabbed the suitcases and I wrangled the animals. Inside, Jimmy sat at the table, nursing a bottle of beer.

"Where's Emma?" I asked.

"She's gone," Jimmy said into his bottle.

I looked between the two men. "Gone?"

"She left a note that she took Heather to the movies, but that was a long time ago," Hudson said. "We've been calling her, but the calls keep going to voicemail."

"Hudson, can I talk to you? Alone?" I asked.

"Sure." He bent down and let Mortiboy out of his carrier, scratched him behind the ears a couple of times, and stood back up. I kept Rocky's leash clipped on and led us to the now-empty guest room.

I sat down on the bed. "Join me?" He sat next to me. Rocky jumped onto the bed and nosed us both before settling down around the pillows. "I know you don't want to hear this, but I don't think Emma is the victim here," I said.

I went on to tell him what I'd started to see: Emma's involvement in the dissemination of information, her connection to Dr. Hall, and her lying about never having been to the motel. If I'd expected him to tell me I was wrong or get angry at me for accusing his sister of being involved in a horrific crime, I would have been disappointed. Hudson wasn't that guy. He also didn't proclaim I was right. He looked at me, his dark brown eyes searching mine, no argument offered, but also no denial or judgment.

"Neither one of us wanted to see it. Emma's painted herself as a victim in all of this, but she could have orchestrated everything that's happened from behind the scenes. The attacks all took place when she wasn't around. So much of what I know came to me from her. She could have made it up to lead me on a wild goose chase."

"But why?"

"Sometimes when people feel trapped, they think there's only one way out of a bad situation." I lowered my voice and reached out for Hudson's hand. "She said Jimmy never hit her, but there are other forms of abuse that aren't physical. I don't know either one of them as well as you do, but no matter what your sister did, I don't think she'd put Heather at risk."

"But if what you're accusing her of is true, then she did. Those drugs we found, they were part of a bigger crime. You think she was working with the doctor to sell them on the street. Drugs, Madison. That's a kind of corruption I can't fathom. If those drugs had hit the street in Salton, a lot of kids might have died."

"There's something else you need to know." I stood up and went into the bathroom, but left the door open. "When we were staying here, I accidentally discovered a stash of pills hidden in the bathroom. Come here."

Hudson stood up and joined me in the tight space. I opened the medicine cabinet. It looked like it had when we were staying here. One by one I removed the contents and set them inside the sink basin, and then I tapped at the shelf until I found a latch that released the fake interior. I slid the metal frame out.

The hidden shelf was empty.

# THIRTY-ONE

"This shelf was full of prescription bottles," I said. "And I mean full. There were probably a hundred vials in here and they're gone. You don't think she took them, do you?"

He slammed the medicine cabinet shut.

Whoever had used this hidden storage area to hide the pills had taken them in the past few days. That meant sometime between Dr. Hall's murder and today, someone involved in the distribution of illegal drugs had been in this house. This bathroom.

It could have been anybody. It could have been Emma or Jimmy. They both lived here. The vials had Emma's name on them but the sheer volume of them was questionable. Did she even know they were there? If so, why hide them?

Now that I'd moved from the house to the Tiki Tropic motel, I had no idea who else had come and gone from the house in the past few days. Was that the real motivation behind the physical assault on Hudson and Jimmy? Benji seemed to be keeping tabs on all of us. Had the attack been a way to keep the guys from the house— Emma and me too—so they could get in and search? Emma had told me that Dr. Hall said he'd left something behind. That was the day of the accident, and it was looking more and more like Dr. Hall had taken pills from Emma's house and then tossed them out his window when we had the accident. But then why leave a full shelf of pills behind? He'd been killed sometime between that accident and the following morning. Had someone been in the house—in this very room—since then?

Hudson left the bathroom while I slid the false shelf back into the interior of the medicine cabinet and then restocked the shelves. When I came out, I was alone. I returned to the dining room and found Jimmy at the table peeling the label off of his bottle of beer. Hudson stood by the sliding doors, staring out into the backyard. I walked over to him and put my arms around him from behind. "If she is involved, she's in danger," I said. "Our number one priority should be to find her and make sure she's okay."

He turned around, surprise and concern on his face. "What about the police?"

"She's your sister and she's Heather's mother. If she did this, then she needs help. Let's find her first and go from there."

"Trust me, she's okay," Jimmy said from behind us. "Emma looks out for one person: Emma."

I got angry. "From what I've seen, she has to. You haven't treated her particularly well. And even now you're just sitting here waiting for her to walk in. She could be in some kind of trouble and you're not even out there looking for her. Why not?"

"Hudson, control your woman," Jimmy said.

"No, I think Madison has a point," Hudson said.

Heat flamed my face and climbed my neck. "Maybe you know more than you're letting on."

Jimmy jumped up from the table, knocking his chair backward. "This is bullshit. I opened my house to you and you've caused me nothing but trouble. Now you're accusing me of something, but I'm not sure what. What do you think I did, Madison? Threatened my wife? Endangered my daughter? Oh, wait, I get it." He took two steps toward me. Even though I was afraid of him and his temper, I stood my ground. "You think I murdered Dr. Hall when I found out he was having an affair with my wife and tossed his body in the river. That's right. You didn't know I knew about that, did you? I saw them together at the antique marketplace. They didn't even try to hide it. Bet that makes me look even more suspicious. But tell me this, miss detective. Why would I dump the body in the same river I'm using as a job site? I'm going bankrupt on this job. You're a businesswoman. Think about this: killing Dr. Hall would have been bad business." He was right in front of me, inches separating us. Hudson stood off to the side, watching but not interfering.

As Jimmy got closer to me, I sensed there more than anger behind his actions. There was frustration. He didn't know what was going on any more than we did. He probably knew less. "What about the hospital? Do you think I beat myself up? And Hudson too?" he asked quietly.

When I replied, I kept my voice low and steady. "The only thing I know here is you are not acting like a concerned father and husband. You're acting helpless and I don't get that. Your wife is missing. Your daughter is too. Maybe they are at the movies, or maybe something very bad happened to them. Why isn't Emma home yet? Why isn't she answering our calls? How come I'm the one asking these questions and you're not?"

"Because Emma made it clear she doesn't want me as a husband. Our marriage has been over for a long time."

# THIRTY-TWO

"We had a trial separation a year ago," Jimmy continued. "After six months, she brought up divorce. I thought we could turn it around. We had Heather to think about. It wasn't just about what Emma wanted anymore."

"So what happened?"

"The usual. We saw a marriage counselor, but it didn't do any good. First session was just Emma accusing me of every single thing I did wrong since saying 'I do.' I sat there and took it, figured she needed to let it all out. But after that, I knew. She had zero interest in working things out. She was laying the groundwork for a new life. I started to suspect that there was somebody else, but when I asked, she told me to stop accusing her. So I laid off."

"Why didn't you say anything?" I asked. "This whole setup—us coming here to work for you, staying at your house, all of it—why even go there?"

"I've been dragging my feet on signing the papers. I know what you're thinking. If I knew Emma was cheating on me, why prolong things?" He looked at me for a second, and then looked Hudson in the eye. "Me and your sister go back a long time. A long time. We've had more rounds than a prize fight. She always came back, man. I had no reason to think this time would be different."

Hudson put his hand on Jimmy's shoulder. "I can't take sides. You know that."

"I know."

The tension was palpable. I excused myself and let the two

men talk. I couldn't help in this matter. I'd been little more than a pawn from the beginning.

I went down the hallway. Mortiboy was asleep on the middle of the bed. I went into the bathroom, turned on the faucet, and washed the dirt and grime I'd picked up from the Middletons' driveway from under my fingernails. I was shaking. Jimmy had made no secret of the fact that he was annoyed with my presence in their house.

The towel grew grimy from dirt left on my knees from earlier. I carried the dirty towel to the hamper where Mortiboy liked to hide and was about to toss it inside when I noticed I'd missed a spot of grime on the outside of my forearm. I wet the corner of the towel, squirted some hand soap onto it, and rubbed at the spot. It didn't come off.

I rubbed a little harder. My flesh turned red with irritation. It took three rounds with the towel and the soap to get the spot clean. That was unlike any dirt I'd encountered before. I held the towel up to my nose and sniffed. The gray spots had a faint clay smell to them, almost unnoticeable under the lemon ginger scent of the hand soap.

I pulled off one of my sneakers and held the sole up to my nose. It smelled like the towel. I reached into the hamper and rooted around for the blue and white towel Mortiboy had been curled up on the day Heather had been missing. It had reddish brown streaks on it and smelled the same. Back in the guest room, I pulled another sneaker out of my luggage and checked the soles. They were clean.

I felt a little nuts sniffing dirty towels and sneaker soles, but something about the stain bothered me. I carried my towel outside and called Hudson over to me.

"Does this smell funny to you?" I asked, holding up the towel.

"Have we already reached that stage of our relationship?"

"I'm serious. It smells like pottery, right?"

"It's clay," Jimmy said from behind Hudson. "We got a lot of clay-rich soil out here. It's so dry around here you find it blowing in the wind. Sometimes won't even notice you picked up a layer until you wash your clothes and see the water runoff."

I stepped away from Hudson and focused on what Jimmy had said. "When you say, 'around here,' do you mean all of Palm Springs?"

"Nope, just pockets. There's some on our street, but not much because the street paved over it. A little on the sides by the property lines. It's bad out by the quarry. Lucky it's been dry. If you get it wet, it's like orange tar."

What Jimmy said made sense. I'd gotten dirty this afternoon while trying to dig the pill vial out from in front of the Middletons' house, and I'd had my yellow sneakers on when I was in the quarry.

"Why are you so worried about a little clay?" Hudson asked.

I held up a dirty towel. "The day Heather was missing, we thought somebody took Mortiboy too. We searched the house and found him in the hamper on a pile of dirty laundry."

"Cats like dark spaces."

I held up the blue and white striped towel Mortiboy had been curled up on. "This towel was underneath him."

"And?" Jimmy asked.

"And it's covered in the same clay I have on my clothes from my day at the quarry. Earlier that day when Emma drove me to the hospital, she had this towel in the car."

"So what?"

I looked at Hudson. "It was clean. Now it's filthy. None of us have been at the quarry. That means Emma has."

"What would she be doing out there? She's not a part of my crew. She doesn't have anything to do with this project."

Even though Jimmy was the one to speak and Hudson had remained quiet, I kept staring at Hudson as though we were the only two there. "Don't you see, Hudson? She's using Jimmy's job as a cover. She's the one Benji was looking for, not me. You wanted proof your sister was at the quarry." I held the towel up. "This is proof."

Hudson took the towel from me. His grip was so tight his

fingers turned white. He stared at it for a couple of seconds, and then looked at Jimmy. "You don't know where she went?"

Jimmy shook his head.

Hudson grabbed the keys. "I can't just sit around here hoping everything's okay. I don't believe my sister killed anybody." He stormed out the front door. I ran after him.

"Where are you going?" I asked.

"To the river. I want to look around and see what we missed."

There were no cars on the road. We turned off the main road mere minutes after leaving the McKennas' driveway. It was late and the entrance to the river was closed by a large metal gate secured in the center with a length of chain and a padlock.

Hudson backed up the Jeep and parked it by the side of the road.

He turned to me. "Are you wearing practical shoes?"

"I live in practical shoes." I climbed out of the car and climbed over the gate. I stopped on the other side and looked back at him. "What are you waiting for?" I asked.

Hudson joined me on the less legal side of the gate and we made quick time to the parking lot. The Avalanche was back, parked in the same space it had occupied earlier in the week.

"I thought Detective Drayton said somebody claimed the key and moved the car?" Hudson asked.

"He did."

The once-shiny SUV had grown dingier in the past two days. I stuck my finger out and dragged it along the passenger side of the car, leaving a streak in the dirt. When I was done, I rubbed my grungy finger against my right hand. The residue transferred and left a spot in the middle of my palm. I rubbed my left thumb against it, but the spot didn't fade.

"It's dirty," Hudson said.

"It's dry dirt. Clay," I said. "Take off your T-shirt." Hudson looked at me like I was out of my mind. "I'd use mine, but it's polyester. Yours is cotton."

"Convenient," he said. He pulled his black T-shirt over his

head and held it out to me. I stood there, temporarily distracted by his bare chest and washboard abs. "Is this what you wanted?"

"It's a nice bonus." I balled his T-shirt up and wiped the side panel of the vehicle, including the windows.

"Hey!"

"It'll wash up nice and new. But look. Now the truck is clean." I pointed to the door. Hudson's brows pulled together and he frowned. I looked at his T-shirt. Clay-colored dirt particles discolored the black fabric. I shook it out and the loose dirt flew off in a cloud around us while the fabric snapped.

"Tell me what you're thinking."

"When we had the accident, the SUV was dirty. The next day, it was clean. But now, when we got here, it was dirty again. After it was moved, this truck went to the quarry. I was so sure the truck belonged to Dr. Hall, but when I heard somebody moved it, I figured I was wrong. Now I don't know what to think."

Hudson pulled on his dirty T-shirt, and then stepped closer to the SUV and pressed his face up against the window. After a second, he pulled out his phone, turned on the flashlight, and aimed it inside.

"Do you see that?" he asked.

I stepped closer and followed the beam of light. It shined into the backseat and landed on Heather's missing stuffed rabbit.

"What's Heather's bunny doing inside the Avalanche?"

Hudson stood up straight and turned to me. "You told the detective about this car, didn't you?"

I nodded. "He told Officer Buchanan to check it out, but when Buchanan came out here for the keys, they were gone and the truck had been moved. With no concrete evidence to tie the two, Drayton wrote it off as coincidence."

"Heather must have been inside the car. Emma put her own daughter at risk." His face grew red and his fists balled up. "She's right in the middle of everything. It's bad enough she got involved with that crooked doctor, but to involve Heather? That's irresponsible."

"She's not thinking clearly," I said. "You heard what Jimmy said. Emma filed for divorce."

"This is grounds for negligence. She could lose custody." He balled up his fist and punched the side of the truck. The fiberglass flexed in and then bounced back.

I reached forward and yanked on the door handle. I don't know what I expected, but I certainly didn't think the door would open. It did. The truck hadn't been locked.

Hudson and I looked at each other. "What the hell?" he asked.

"The night we got here, Heather was upset because she couldn't find her stuffed bunny. Emma told me she'd been crying all day until Rocky and Mortiboy arrived."

"But why would Heather's bunny be in Dr. Hall's car?" Hudson asked. He reached into the backseat and grabbed the bunny. He stood there, next to the SUV, the bunny still in his grip. He stared at the small plush face as though searching for answers. I put my hand on his arm.

"There's another explanation," I offered. He searched my face for answers. I could see a form of desperation there, hope that whatever I said would cast his sister's recent actions in a better light. Unfortunately, the better light was fraught with a whole other set of problems. "Emma saw Dr. Hall leave the house with two duffle bags. Ernie had the one filled with pills. It's possible that Dr. Hall took the bunny as insurance—or leverage—or whatever you call it. Something to scare Emma into seeing that he could get to her little girl if she made trouble for him." I squeezed Hudson's hands. "Emma searched the house for that bunny. I honestly don't think she knew it was in this truck."

"This isn't about the bunny," Hudson said. "It's about Emma. Where is she? Why isn't she out here with us, helping to find out what happened?"

"Because maybe she's in trouble."

# THIRTY-THREE

The color drained from his face. I squeezed his arm to comfort him. Valuable seconds ticked past while we stood there, not speaking, barely touching, Hudson lost as to how to help his sister, me lost in how to help Hudson.

Headlights cut through the night. It was too dark to make out the car that approached, but there seemed to be no question it was headed our direction. We'd had to abandon our car and proceed on foot. If the person headed our way was acting in some official manner, they'd likely be able to bypass the gate.

The headlights stopped at about the location where our car was parked.

"We should call the police," I said.

"That might be the police."

The headlights cut off. A car door slammed. We didn't move. About twenty seconds later, the lights went back on and the car jumped backward in an arc. The car pulled forward and completed a U-turn, then picked up speed on its way out of the park.

"I don't think that was the police." I grabbed Hudson's hand and pulled him forward with me. "I left my handbag in the car. We have to leave. They probably know who we are. It's not safe."

Hudson shoved the bunny at me and ran toward the car. I followed him, but couldn't keep up. He started the Jeep and swung it around in a semi-circle like the other car but waited for me. I tossed the bunny inside the open window and climbed inside. I felt around on the seat and the floorboards for my handbag. It—including my phone and my ID—was gone. Whoever had followed us to the river knew I was still looking for answers. Hudson slammed his foot down and the tires spun for a second before catching on the loose gravel and dirt and propelling us forward.

We tore past the gates of the park. Hudson closed the gap between us and the other car and flashed his lights. There was no misunderstanding our intent, but still, the car in front of us sped on. I didn't tell Hudson my newest theory because it had a frightening reality to it. More frightening than the alternatives we'd suspected so far. There was one other way Heather's bunny could have ended up in the back of the Avalanche.

Aside from the occasional "there he is," "he switched lanes," and "quick, turn left," there wasn't much conversation in the car. It was more civilized than the high-speed chases you saw on TV, probably because both cars involved had a reason to avoid being pulled over by the police.

I wasn't clear on whether or not the car in front of us knew we were following it until our chase turned onto a road which turned into little more than a dirt path for off-road vehicles. In front of us, a crane stood next to a construction site. The sign announced new luxury condos. We were at the construction site behind Emma and Jimmy's house. The car in front of us drove at a breakneck speed, headed for a spot between the crane and the poured foundation.

"That area is dangerous," I said. "They just poured the foundation a few days ago. It's probably not even set. I don't know anything about concrete, but will it hold the weight of a car?"

"We're about to find out."

As we got closer to the job site, the car approached the crane. From a distance, I couldn't tell if the small car had enough clearance to make it through the gap. If it did, it would get away. No way would our Jeep be able to follow.

Hudson slowed the car to a stop. "I have a bad feeling about this," he said.

The car in front of us eased through the opening. I expected the driver to accelerate immediately, to drive between the rows of houses to the dirt road and then back out to the main road of Palm

Springs. We were only a handful of miles from Highway 111, and with the light traffic and a head start, he'd lose us easily. But the car didn't speed up. It slowed and then stopped.

"What's happening?" I asked.

"I don't know. Wait here." Hudson got out of the Jeep and crept forward into the darkness. When he got about twenty feet in front of me, his silhouette faded into the darkness. I picked up his outline when he crept in front of the partially constructed building. I strained my eyes, trying to make out what was happening. It was too quiet. We'd been led here like mice trailing a piece of cheese. It didn't make sense the person who lured us here would be sitting quietly in the car, waiting for Hudson to approach.

And then I saw another figure disappear around the other side of the crane. Hudson was walking into a trap.

I undid my seatbelt and opened the car door. An interior light went on. I grabbed Hudson's black bandana from the center console and threw it over the interior light. The only edge we might have was if the driver of the sports car thought there was only one of us. Announcing my presence with the car seemed unwise. I had nothing—no plan, no weapon, no phone. We were the length of an Olympic-sized swimming pool from Emma and Jimmy's house, and if I could get there undetected, I could call for help.

I eased the door shut and left it resting next to the latch. I crept forward, keeping to the shadows. Hudson had taken an almost direct path between the Jeep and the sports car, the shortest distance between two points. Now that I'd gotten closer, I could see his silhouette next to the car. I reached the crane and flattened myself against it, slowly moving along the side. Every couple of seconds I looked up to make sure Hudson was okay. I reached the end of the crane and peeked around the other side. The muzzle of a gun equipped with a silencer slowly extended past the edge, pointed in Hudson's direction.

# THIRTY-FOUR

I had one chance at the element of surprise. I took a deep breath and screamed as loud as I could.

The gun went off. Hudson cried out. The sports car shuddered with the impact of a bullet. A figure dressed in black ran from the side of the crane toward the line of houses.

I ran to Hudson and dropped down next to him. "Are you okay?"

"Yes," he said. "The bullet nicked my arm and went into the car. Did you call the police?"

"My handbag is missing from the car. I think whoever shot you stole it."

"My phone's in my pocket. Can you get to it?"

I felt down the outside of his jeans pockets until I located the rectangular outline of his phone, and then reached my hand in wriggled it around until my fingers closed around it. He gave me a feeble smile.

"Is that what you wanted?" I asked, keeping my tone light.

"It's a nice bonus," he said. He smiled, but I could tell the effort hurt.

The screen of his phone was shattered. "It's dead," I said.

"Get to Emma's and call the cops. I'll be okay. Go."

I stood up and took two steps away from him and then doubled back. "I won't leave you."

I bent down, putting my hands under Hudson's arms. He dug his heels into the ground and pushed, and together we moved him backward until he was up against the sports car. I grabbed the door handle and yanked it open. A tumble of papers fell out. I tried to kick them away, but one stuck to my shoe. "Get inside," I said. "You'll be less vulnerable than if you're out here exposed."

"I'm good. You have to go."

I dropped to a squat and took his face in my hands. "I'll be right back," I said. I leaned forward and kissed him, and then, just as my knee screamed out in agony, stood up and ran toward the exterior of the closest house. I crept forward, sticking to the shadows. It wasn't until I tripped the floodlight outside Jo's house that I saw there was blood covering my arms, hands, and feet. Hudson's blood.

There was no time to spare for tears over whether or not he would be okay. The only way for me to save him was to get to the house and get help. I cut across the front of Jo's yard and ran to Emma's front door. It was locked. I rang the bell over and over and then pounded on the door.

Jo's hatchback pulled into her driveway. She turned off the lights and got out. "Madison, is that you? Is everything okay?"'

I stood back from the door. "No, everything isn't okay. Have you seen Jimmy or Emma? Is Heather with you?"

"I haven't seen anybody. I'm just getting home from the concert hall. I thought I was a mess because of the makeup, but you're worse. What is that—chocolate?"

I looked down at my clothes, stained dark red from my contact with Hudson after he was shot. "I need to use your phone. Can I use your phone?"

"Sure, sure," she said. She reached into her handbag. "My cell always gets lost in here. Hold on."

I walked toward her. Something was stuck to my left sneaker sole. I put my hand on the hood of her car for balance and lifted my foot to peel the paper off. It was an ad for Jo's concert series that she'd probably dropped earlier.

I crumpled the paper into a ball. That's when I noticed the blood.

This flyer hadn't been dropped earlier. It had fallen out of the car Hudson was resting against. The blood was Hudson's. But if the flyer had fallen out of the car, that meant the driver had been Jo.

It had been Jo. All along, everything that had happened. Jo had been the driver. Jo had been the shooter. Jo had been the person who'd been running prescription drugs under everybody's noses.

Jo was a murderer. She'd killed her ex-husband. And now she'd shot Hudson.

I glanced in the car. The keys were still dangling from the ignition column. Slowly, I looked up at her. Her face, made up in garish stage makeup, looked grotesque under the floodlights. She held her handbag in one hand, her other hand concealed by the interior. I had a feeling she wasn't holding her cell phone.

"Cute trick back there," she said. "Your scream startled me just enough to make me lose aim." She shrugged. "Maybe he'll bleed out," she said, as if she were talking about the odds it would rain. "I'm not much for predictions, but I don't think the same thing is going to happen twice."

"Where's Emma?"

"Probably at the movie theater waiting on the girls. I told her to meet me there. Now she and Jimmy can waste the rest of the night pretending to get along while I wrap up things here."

"I thought you had a performance tonight?"

"Sore throat," she said. "My understudy was happy to step in. Lucky for me she left her keys in the dressing room. Not sure how happy she'll be when she finds out about the bullet hole in the side of her car though."

"But your car—where did you come from?"

"Try to keep up, would you, Madison? If you'd seen my car in my driveway earlier, you would have known I was home. I parked it at the end of the lane."

"And you drove back here so you could pretend to just be getting home. The stage makeup is all part of your story. You killed your ex-husband because he stood between you and the pills."

"I killed him because he destroyed my life. He was supposed to deliver the pills to me that morning. He had the bag and it looked full. It wasn't until I looked inside and saw the stuffed bunny that I realized he tricked me. He weighted the bag down with buckshot. The last thing he said after taking the overdose was that Emma had the pills. Sweet little Emma who never recognized that Albert was just using her, and not for sex. He laughed in my face right before I pushed him into the river. I thought I'd take the bunny back to their house, and then play the comforting friend. Help poor Emma through her divorce. But then they have house guests—you. People going through divorce don't suddenly get hit with the desire to be hospitable."

"That's why you encouraged me—us—to get a room at the motel," I said. "You wanted us out of the way so you could search for the drugs. You're the one who slipped the note into my towel."

"Technically Benji left you the note after I told him where to find you."

"Did you send him to the quarry too? And to Salton to attack Jimmy and Hudson?"

"Benji was the only one who knew I killed Albert. I told him Albert's body was in the river and to make it disappear. Nobody counted on you seeing his face in the water or calling the police before Benji finished the job. When the police notified me of Albert's death, I found out what they knew. You were a loose end. I told Benji to watch you, and if you made trouble, to make you disappear too. He should have taken care of you by the quarry. He told me you wandered off by yourself. Benji's not known for his kind heart and generous nature."

Hearing her say with extreme calm that she'd sent thugs to our motel to kill me let me know how far gone Jo Conway really was. It also filled me with fear. Anyone who could talk about murder in such a completely detached voice was already beyond the point of having something to lose. If Jo had nothing to lose, then there was little I could do to distract her. But the image of Hudson, shot and bleeding in the construction site behind the property line, stayed with me.

"Albert was an idiot. He had a nice little thing going, selling prescription pills on the street. But then he has a crisis of conscience and stopped. What he didn't realize was that there's a simple law of supply and demand. As soon as the police department declared war on drugs, drugs became a lot more valuable. Albert had amassed a lot of inventory when he was selling. He wrote bogus prescriptions and sat on a mountain of pharmaceutical samples. It wasn't hard to drain his stash, not at first. And after I stole his prescription pad, I thought I was home free. The genius of my plan was I never got greedy. A couple of pills sold here and there was enough to make up for his indiscretions."

I thought of the bags of pills Ernie Middleton had found on the side of the road. "But you did get greedy, didn't you? I saw the bags of pills. That wasn't a pill here and there. There were enough to mess up a lot of people."

"Albert figured out what I was doing and he freaked. He moved his stash. If he really wanted to fix the problem he would have destroyed all of those pills, but he wanted to be a hero. He was going to plant the pills and then be part of the bust."

"He hid the pills at Emma's house," I said. "Some in a secret compartment behind her medicine cabinet, and probably more elsewhere. She saw him from your kitchen and went over to talk. That's why he was in such a hurry when he left. He caused our accident that first day, trying to get out of there before you noticed him. All he wanted was to keep you from getting your hands on them."

I'd wondered about the sheer volume of pills Ernie had found and I'd been suspicious of Emma because the pills had been in her cabinet. Albert must have hidden the prescription drugs in pill vials until he could move them. If what Jo was telling me was true, then I'd known about the pills before Emma had. The day she saw Albert at her house—the day Hudson and I arrived—must have been the day Albert realized what his ex-wife was doing. He'd gone to Emma's house to hide the pills, but when Emma told him we were coming to stay, when she broke things off, he needed a plan B. That was the day he'd almost run us off the road. The day the bags of pills had ended up in the Middletons' driveway. Whether he'd been planning a bait and switch all along or if the idea came to him spontaneously, we'd never know. But it looked now as though he tossed the duffel bag with the pills out of his truck when we came around the bend—possibly to recover later—and took the duffel bag with the bunny to the pier.

"What now, Jo? Are you going to shoot me? Right here in the driveway? How are you going to explain it to your daughter when she gets home? That there's a dead woman in front of your house? Or do you have a plan to dispose of me too?"

I stood on the opposite side of her hatchback. Her handbag rested on the hood, and she'd relaxed both arms while answering my questions. She was distracted. It was my only chance.

Before she could answer, I dropped to a crouch. Pain speared my knee. I yanked the door open and dove in to the car. The keys dangled from the ignition column. I flipped them and the engine caught. I jammed the car into reverse. Jo aimed the gun at the windshield. I ducked down and pressed my hand onto the gas pedal. The windshield shattered as the car lurched backward. Seconds later, it slammed into something. My head ricocheted forward and then back and the world turned black.

# THIRTY-FIVE

I opened my eyes and stared into the face of Ernie Middleton. It took a moment to realize his odd coloring was due to the blue and red lights flashing behind him. I tried to sit up and he pushed me back down.

"Settle down, missy. Everything's under control. You got banged up pretty good back there. Cops are taking care of things now. Medics checked you out and said you're going to be okay. Right now, you rest."

"But Hudson's out back."

"Your boyfriend? Nope, he's over there talking to Officer Buchanan." He stood up and snapped his fingers at an EMT standing nearby. "Hey! A little help over here. She's conscious." Ernie sat back down in a folding aluminum beach chair next to me.

"Did I back into your car?"

"Yep. Ever since the cops lectured me about those pills, I've been keeping watch on the neighborhood. Saw two cars driving like teenagers at the construction site out behind your house. I got into my own car so I could get a closer look. You came right at me. Lost a couple of years when I didn't see anybody behind the wheel."

"I'm sorry."

"I'm not. I keep telling Eunice it's time for a new car. No excuses now."

I closed my eyes and felt myself falling back into darkness. When I heard my name, I fought to open my eyes.

Detective Drayton stood over me. "Ms. Night," he said. "You're a lucky woman."

I put my fingers to my forehead. The skin was tender and raised in a lump by my hairline. "What happened?"

"Not sure anybody knows the full story. When you're recovered, we'll get your statement. Right now we're going to move you to the hospital with Mr. James."

"Is he okay?"

"He lost some blood, but he'll be fine."

"Did you catch her? Jo Conway?"

"We took her into custody while you were out."

"How'd you know?" I looked at Ernie. "Did you call the police when I hit you?"

Drayton cleared his throat. "Mr. Middleton may have had something to do with detaining Ms. Conway until we arrived, but Officer Buchanan was the one who figured it out. We were already on our way when your accident took place."

There was so much I didn't know, but all I wanted was to close my eyes and go to sleep for a long, long time.


Rocky's cold, wet nose nudged my fingertips. I opened my eyes and stroked his fur. It took a moment to realize that I was in the guest bedroom of Jimmy and Emma's house. I woke naturally, not screaming over memories or groggy from drugs. Mortiboy was on the opposite side of my legs from Rocky, his paws curled up underneath him and his black kitty head resting on my calf. His eyes were closed and the smooth fur of his body raised and dropped evenly. If there was a scrapbook of cherished moments from our lives waiting for us in Heaven, I sure hoped a photo of this would be included.

"Hey, Lady," Hudson said. I turned my head and smiled. He rested against the door frame, the man in black surrounded by white molding. A white bandage protruded from underneath the sleeve of his right bicep. "Looks like your trouble with sleep is over. I was starting to wonder if it was going to take a kiss from a prince to wake you up."

"Wouldn't hurt, just to be on the safe side," I said. "Come here."

Hudson crossed the room and sat on the edge of the bed. Mortiboy opened his eyes and raised his head. Hudson ran his hand over his cat, and then picked up my hand and held it. He bent down and kissed me gently.

"You going to make it?"

"I will now," I said. "Can you tell me what happened? The detective said Buchanan was the one who figured it out. How? And how did they know you were behind the houses? Where did Jimmy go? And Benji. Did they catch him too?"

"Whoa, slow down. There's plenty of time for all of your questions."

"Humor me. Right now there's not much more I can do other than ask questions."

"You've got a point." He gingerly touched my forehead and eased his hand down the side of my face. He ran his thumb back and forth over my lips and I kissed it, then raised my hand and moved it away.

"Stop trying to distract me," I said.

He laughed. "Okay. Understand this is a Frankenstein version of the story because I've had to piece it together from a whole lot of sources. Nobody knows the whole thing."

"Understood."

"Jo must have jumped out of the car after reaching the construction site. She thought you were the one driving—that you were the one she was aiming at. When you screamed from right next to her, you took her by surprise. She lost her aim and the bullet only grazed me."

"I know what happened after that. After I left you, I ran to the house to call for help. Jimmy was gone and their house was locked up. I was about to break in when Jo pulled in next door. If I had broken in and called the cops, none of this would have happened."

"If you had broken in and called the cops, she would have gotten away."

"She admitted to everything," I said. "She killed her husband. She sent Benji to scare me at the quarry and to jump you and Jimmy in Salton. Dr. Hall had the stuffed bunny in his duffel bag instead of the pills. He filled the bag with buckshot so it would appear heavy and full. After Jo killed him, she took the bunny. She thought it would be a good excuse to get back into the house to search for the pills. She put the threatening note in my towel. The day Heather was in the park, that was all orchestrated by Jo to get Emma out of the house, but then I showed up and ruined her plan."

He stroked the side of my face again. "You sure you want to talk about this?"

I nodded. "I want closure," I said. I rearranged myself as best as I could, sitting up against the pillows. "Detective Drayton said something about Buchanan figuring everything out. How?"

"He said he kept thinking about the day he came over with Rock, the day Heather was missing. Emma said Jo usually picked up the girls, but Jo said she pulled Gina out of school early so she could get to rehearsal. Buchanan checked with the orchestra. There was no rehearsal that day. He went back to the school to question the vice principal, who said it wasn't prearranged like Jo said. Jo showed up and pulled Gina out of the middle of her last class."

"You and Jimmy got into that fight in Salton. She wasn't counting on that. She had to do damage control—keep us from asking questions about you by making up a bigger threat with Heather."

I'd wondered about that day. I'd brought it up to Tex, right before I told him I didn't trust Buchanan. And Buchanan was the one who followed up on the detail and saved us all.

"What about the truck by the river?"

"The SUV was rented to Dr. Hall. Nobody knows the truth, but it looks like he might have jammed those keys between the pier slats himself to draw attention to the car, just like you thought."

"But it didn't work. If I had never noticed the keys, the car would have been impounded within a week. That's what Lora told me." I closed my eyes and thought about the park ranger and how she'd told little Heather she was lucky not to have an older brother. "Lora, the park ranger—she was Benji's sister, wasn't she?"

Hudson nodded. "After the news picked up the story of Jo's involvement in the drug ring, Lora went to the police and told them where to find Benji. She said she was tired of looking the other way when it came to him."

"If it hadn't been for us and the car accident when we arrived, Jo and Benji would have spent that week looking for the drugs."

"They could have hurt Ernie and Eunice Middleton."

"They *did* hurt you," I said. "How do you feel?"

"Alive," he said.

We were both silent for a few moments. Dr. Hall had been no prince, but he'd tried to change, to undo the bad he'd done, and it had cost him his life.

"So what now?" I asked.

"I'm going to stick around a little longer and try to get Jimmy back on schedule. He and Emma are going to try counseling again, but it's going to be an uphill battle."

"What's going to happen to Gina, Jo's daughter?"

"She's going to live with her grandparents," he said.

"Just like you did when your parents died."

He nodded. "Here's hoping she has the same bond with hers I had with mine."

"What's going to happen to us?" I asked. He was quiet for a few seconds. He looked out the window over my head, and then down at the thin blanket covering me. His lack of eye contact worried me. "Hudson? We both kept secrets from each other this past week. Are we okay?"

"Yeah, we're good. And a part of me wants to pack up and run away with you and try to forget any of this every happened."

"But?"

"But I can't leave my sister here with Jimmy. Not now. We both saw the anger in their relationship. Maybe they'll work things out, maybe they won't. I want to believe Emma is a grown woman who can take care of herself, but she's not like you, Madison. She's never been alone a day in her life. I'll let her make her own decisions, but I don't want her making them based on a need for security or a fear of change."

I looked down at Rocky, who stared back at me with his big pleading brown eyes. His face rested on the blanket, his fur fluffed out underneath him. He looked like he was thinking the same thing I was.

"I can't set up camp in Palm Springs indefinitely," I said. "I know we said two weeks, but this trip took a lot more out of me than I expected. I don't want to live my life afraid to fall asleep because of the nightmares, and the longer I stay away from home, the harder it's going to be to face those memories and get past them. I don't think I can solve this problem on my own."

"I know."

"I guess Emma doesn't want to come with you to Texas?"

"That's her running away, not dealing with her problems. Just like before. She has to face the music."

I looked from Rocky to Hudson. This time he was looking back at me. "I don't think our first getaway happened under the best of circumstances," I said. "What we had in Dallas was great and I wouldn't trade it for anything, but this trip wasn't exactly a positive endorsement for long-term commitment."

"Not a lot of love lost among the people we spent our time with, was there?"

"Nope." I moved my hand and grasped his fingers and squeezed. "I don't want to be in a relationship like that. I never want to feel so trapped that I purposely hurt someone I love."

"Me neither." He reached down and brushed a few stray blonde hairs out of my face with his rough fingertips. "You know what Doris Day would say at a time like this, don't you?"

I smiled. "The future's not ours to see. Que sera, sera."

# EPILOGUE

*Tex*

Tex recognized the number on his phone before he answered it. Palm Springs Police Department. Thanks to his scanner and the various updates on social media, he already knew what had gone down. The call, he assumed, was a courtesy.

"Tex Allen," he answered.

"Captain Allen, it's Officer Buchanan. Thought you'd want to know how things worked out." Buchanan gave him the rundown of events. "Your friends are going to be okay. Not sure how much longer they're going to stay out here, but I think it's pretty safe to say they're going to lay low for the rest of their vacation."

Friends? Were he and Hudson James ever going to be friends? Probably not. But now they were both official members of the "I got shot because of Madison Night" club. Guess that counted for something.

"Thanks, I appreciate the phone call. You guys did a good job out there. Biggest drug bust in Palm Springs history, I heard."

"Yeah, Narco Task Force is pretty happy. So's Detective Drayton. It's a good day to be a cop." Buchanan was silent for a beat. "Listen, Captain, I know you didn't want me to say anything, but I owe you a big thank you for looking into the orchestra rehearsal the day little Heather was missing. I don't think anybody would have questioned Ms. Conway's story. That's what got me out there the night everything went down. Your hunch probably saved both of your friends' lives."

Tex had had no justifiable reason to check it out. He'd

explained it to Buchanan as a hunch, but he knew Peter would have a field day with it in their next therapy session.

Tex closed the door to his office. "Nobody needs to know about that, especially not Madison Night."

"She knows everything else about the case. Considering the outcome, I don't think she'd mind."

"This time I think it's best to keep her in the dark. Remember what we agreed. This whole conversation stays between you and me."

## Diane Vallere

After two decades working for a top luxury retailer, Diane Vallere traded fashion accessories for accessories to murder. She is a Lefty Best Humorous Mystery Nominee and, in addition to the Madison Night series, writes the Material Witness and Style & Error mysteries. Diane started her own detective agency at age ten and has maintained a passion for shoes, clues, and clothes ever since. Visit her at www.dianevallere.com.

**The Madison Night Mystery Series
by Diane Vallere**

<u>Novels</u>

PILLOW STALK (#1)

THAT TOUCH OF INK (#2)

WITH VICS YOU GET EGGROLL (#3)

THE DECORATOR WHO KNEW TOO MUCH (#4)

<u>Novellas</u>

MIDNIGHT ICE
(in OTHER PEOPLE'S BAGGAGE)

## Henery Press Mystery Books

And finally, before you go...
Here are a few other mysteries
you might enjoy:

# TELL ME NO LIES

Lynn Chandler Willis

## An Ava Logan Mystery (#1)

Ava Logan, single mother and small business owner, lives deep in the heart of the Appalachian Mountains, where poverty and pride reign. As publisher of the town newspaper, she's busy balancing election season stories and a rash of ginseng thieves.

And then the story gets personal. After her friend is murdered, Ava digs for the truth all the while juggling her two teenage children, her friend's orphaned toddler, and her own muddied past. Faced with threats against those closest to her, Ava must find the killer before she, or someone she loves, ends up dead.

Available at booksellers nationwide and online

Visit www.henerypress.com for details

# MURDER ON A SILVER PLATTER

Shawn Reilly Simmons

## A Red Carpet Catering Mystery (#1)

Penelope Sutherland and her Red Carpet Catering company just got their big break as the on-set caterer for an upcoming blockbuster. But when she discovers a dead body outside her house, Penelope finds herself in hot water. Things start to boil over when serious accidents threaten the lives of the cast and crew. And when the film's star, who happens to be Penelope's best friend, is poisoned, the entire production is nearly shut down.

Threats and accusations send Penelope out of the frying pan and into the fire as she struggles to keep her company afloat. Before Penelope can dish up dessert, she must find the killer or she'll be the one served up on a silver platter.

Available at booksellers nationwide and online

Visit www.henerypress.com for details

# CROPPED TO DEATH

Christina Freeburn

## A Faith Hunter Scrap This Mystery (#1)

Former US Army JAG specialist, Faith Hunter, returns to her West Virginia home to work in her grandmothers' scrapbooking store determined to lead an unassuming life after her adventure abroad turned disaster. But her quiet life unravels when her friend is charged with murder—and Faith inadvertently supplied the evidence. So Faith decides to cut through the scrap and piece together what really happened.

With a sexy prosecutor, a determined homicide detective, a handful of sticky suspects and a crop contest gone bad, Faith quickly realizes if she's not careful, she'll be the next one cropped.

Available at booksellers nationwide and online

Visit www.henerypress.com for details

Printed in Great Britain
by Amazon